The Legend of See Bird:

The Last Long Drive

by

Karl L. Stewart

Don enjoy the book,

Karl L. Stewart

Publisher Page

an imprint of Headline Books, Inc.

Terra Alta, WV

The Legend of See Bird: The Last Long Drive

by Karl L. Stewart

copyright ©2012 Karl L. Stewart

To order additional copies of this book,
or for book publishing information, or to contact the author:

Headline Books, Inc.
P.O. Box 52
Terra Alta, WV 26764
www.headlinebooks.com

Tel: 800-570-5951
Email: mybook@headlinebooks.com

Publisher Page is an imprint of Headline Books

ISBN-13: 978-0-938467-28-1

Library of Congress Control Number: 2012934241

Stewart, Karl L.
The Legend of See Bird / by Karl L. Stewart
   p.cm.
ISBN 978-0-938467-28-1
1. Native American Indians--US--Fiction. 2. Choctaw--Fiction 3. Cattle
Drives--Fiction

PRINTED IN THE UNITED STATES OF AMERICA

Dedication

To my great-grandfather—
my original Western hero

Chapter 1

The old Indian slipped through the long, late summer grass in his characteristic crouch, placing one silent step before another, in a pattern learned so long ago it was now an ingrained habit that would have required a conscious effort on his part to alter. To a knowing observer, the nondescript, uncreased black slouch hat drawn low on his head would have identified him not just as a Choctaw, but his clan and the area he came from as well. His dark eyes flicked left, right, then slowly back to his left. What might have been the start of a smile tightened his lips and deepened the crow's feet at the corners of his eyes. Certain that the soft cooing, almost humming, now gone silent, lay just over there, he reached one hand behind him, palm open.

The young boy, following in See Bird's footsteps, had neither heard nor seen anything of notice. He was conscious only of the thrill of the hunt and the need for stealth. Just once since they left the farmhouse had the old man turned his face the boy's way, when the child had by accident stepped on and snapped a dry twig. See Bird had said not a word, but the boy had blushed furiously and averted his eyes in shame.

He treasured the time spent with his great-grandfather. His reverence for the old man bordered on awe. Few words passed between them, but to the boy, few were needed. The two seemed to be in constant conversation. He spent many evenings sitting on the weathered grey plank porch step, begging Granny to tell him stories of the "old days," of cowboys and rodeos and bucking broncs. He never asked directly about "Grand-Dad" because, if he had, See Bird would have slowly risen from where he sat, carefully set aside the knife and piece of wood he had been whittling into some western shape, brush the wood chips off the front of his overalls, and walk silently away.

Now, the old man froze and extended his hand behind him like a relay racer poised for the baton pass. The boy halted as well and leaned forward to place the .22 caliber rifle in the palm of the extended leathery-brown hand. In his excitement, the child realized he had been holding his breath. He exhaled with a soft sigh. The grass to their immediate front left erupted with the pounding of wings as a flock of pheasants scattered into the air. The boy dropped the rifle and covered his head in shock. See Bird just stood a bit straighter and pointed the index finger of his right hand at a low-flying bird. "Bang," was all he said. The boy could scarcely believe what happened next. The large bird instantly ceased flapping its wings and tumbled to the ground scarcely a dozen feet away, as if shot dead. He stood with his mouth agape as the old man approached the crumpled bird. See Bird looked at the bird. He looked at his finger. Then he looked at the boy and back to his still pointed finger. "It never done that before," was all he said, and he bent to retrieve the bird. As he walked by the still immobile boy, he said, "It's okay. You saved me a bullet. Let's go home." The boy stared at the back of the old man, and picking up the rifle, turned to follow. It's true, he thought. Grand-dad does have magic hands.

Although it had been a while since it had last evidenced itself, the idea there was magic in his hands did not surprise See Bird at all. As he and the boy returned to the farm house, he remembered back to a home, now so long ago and far away to the west. He and his twin brother See Right were fishing in the Kiamichi River that flowed not a half mile from their log and stucco home. It had been a very hot day, he remembered, much hotter than this day, and the two seven-year-olds had been counting the days until they would be allowed to start attending the small nearby Presbyterian mission school. Perhaps it was the heat; perhaps it was that the fish just weren't biting. Whatever the cause, the two youngsters looked at each other and in an instant, came to an unspoken agreement. In seconds both of them had shed their few garments, abandoned their cane poles on the stream bank, and squealing with laughter, launched themselves head first into the cooling waters.

Both boys were already excellent swimmers—See Bird, small and lithe, cut through the water like a trout. His twin, See Right, though larger, was also stronger, and would pull away from his brother when they raced longer distances, either on land or in the water.

"See Right, look at me!" the smaller of the twins shouted. "This is how you look when you dive, like the dog." With a mischievous squeal, he threw himself off the bank, barely three feet above the muddy water and raised a surprisingly large splash as he belly-flopped into the stream.

"Hah!" the other said as he clambered up the muddy bank to stand on the spot his brother had just vacated. "And this is how you look when you dive, like a rock." At that, he executed a grotesque copy of his brother knifing into the water, plunging down at an unfamiliar and awkward angle.

See Bird laughed to see his brother floundering and churning up the water even more. *That is a terrible imitation of me*, he thought. *My dives never look that clumsy*. Even as he was completing that thought, warning alarms rang in his head. See Right was struggling to stand, struggling and falling back into the water, only to fight his way back to his feet again. Clearly, something had gone badly wrong. See Bird lunged through the water to where his brother, hacking and sputtering, had gained his feet once more. "My arm, my arm," he coughed. "I hit it when I dived. I think it must be broken." See Bird wrapped his arms around his brother's waist and helped him up out of the water. Once on shore, the two boys collapsed on the ground, See Right moaning in agony as pain jolted his small body. "Go get help," he pleaded. "I can't walk with this. Every time I move it hurts worse." With that he fell backwards onto the grass with a cry.

See Bird felt lost in a whirl of indecision. He didn't want to leave his brother, but clearly something had to be done quickly. Every time See Right struggled to sit up, he would collapse again crying out in pain. Without thinking about what he was doing, only that he needed to help, he found his small fingers working his injured brother's arm, tenderly kneading and massaging upward from the wrist, working steadily to the shoulder. "Brother, I don't think it is broken."

"What are you talking about? It hurts so bad, I can't move it."

"I know. It doesn't feel right to me either, but I think you knocked the shoulder out of its place. If you let me, I think I could put it back in."

"Please stop the pain."

See Bird stopped biting his lower lip and reached a decision. "Okay," he said as he positioned himself by his brother's injured side. As he spoke he carefully held his brother's wrist. "I'm going to pull out your arm even further and twist it back into its place. It will probably hurt more. Can you bear it?"

Something in the way See Bird spoke, his confidence, seemed to affect See Right, to calm his fear. "Yes, I can. Be quick, please, brother." Without saying another word, the boy slipped his hand up his brother's arm, past the elbow and gripped hard. He placed his brown feet against his brother's side and bent his back, like an oarsman set to stroke. "Do it now," See Right pleaded. "I can't wait any more."

Braced so, See Bird suddenly yanked backwards, turning the arm as he did. The other boy yelled once in pain and then fell silent. See Bird released the arm, and his brother flexed the fingers. Tentatively, he bent the arm and drew it to his side. Even as he did so, the pain subsided into a dull soreness and then receded even more. He looked at See Bird's face, seeing in his brother's eyes all the hope and anxiety he felt for him, and noticed in himself a new feeling welling up alongside the ever present brotherly affection and rivalry, a sense of deep respect. "How did you know what to do?" he asked as he sat up, still clutching his arm. "How did you know how to fix it?"

See Bird shrugged, relieved to see his brother no longer in pain. "I don't know," he said. "It just seemed the right thing to do." He smiled, carefree again, "Who cares? It worked." He rose and reached for his brother's hand. See Right almost reached out with his right hand before he pulled it back and extended his left.

"No," he said. "You have healed it. I must not be afraid to use it." With that, he grasped his brother's hand with his recently injured arm and rose to his feet. The two small boys retrieved their fishing poles and turned for home. They walked in silence for a few minutes, each lost in his own thoughts. "See Bird," the other said, "I have heard there are men of our people who can do such things. I think you may have magic hands."

See Bird said nothing. He too had heard the stories, but whether or not they were as true as the Bible stories he had been learning, he didn't know. And he really didn't care either. All that really mattered, he thought, as he watched their copper feet kicking up dust along the dry path, was that See Right was okay. He smiled again to himself at the thought.

Turning a corner of the path, the boys spied the familiar cottonwoods and oak. Nestled in their speckled shadows squatted their home—and something else, a horse and buggy. "Look, See Right, we've got company."

The boys stopped in their tracks and stared a moment. "I know that wagon," See Right said, "It's Uncle Isaac. C'mon." With that the two raced forward. Perhaps it was the short distance, perhaps See Right's arm still hurt. Whatever the reason, See Bird called out, "I win," as he touched the wagon side several strides ahead of his brother and stopped to catch his breath. But See Right had not even slowed down.

"Uncle Isaac, Uncle Isaac," he called as he dashed past the wagon and into the house, colliding with the lean man who was just emerging. Isaac clutched the boy on the rebound.

"Whoa there, young fella. What's all this commotion?" He squatted and gave the boy a hug. "Now where is your shadow? Ah, here he is," he laughed, as See Bird leaped on his back, wrapping his skinny arms around his uncle's neck. "I think I found him."

Uncle Isaac was a favorite of the two boys. Their mother's older brother, he had led a life full of danger and excitement. He was a warrior descended from warriors. When The War Between The States had broken out, Grey Hawk had joined a band of other young Choctaw men who had fought as a unit of the Confederate cavalry. The family had heard little of him for months at a time. Once he wrote and told them he changed his name to Isaac. They had not known what to make of that, though name changing was a common practice. When the war ended and no word was received and other men from the area trickled back, they began to fear the worst. It was on a late summer afternoon, much like this day, that Abbie spied a lone and dusty horseman approaching their house. She didn't recognize the rider at first but something about the set of the shoulders seemed familiar. It was only when the man called out, "Halito," and raised his hand in greeting and she tried to reciprocate that she finally recognized her brother. She tried, but when she lifted her hand, stabbing pains lanced through her abdomen, swollen with the child she had been carrying for nine months now. "Grey Hawk," she moaned as she slumped against the door frame.

Before she could collapse completely, she was swept up into her brother's arms and carried indoors, where he laid her on her bed. "I'm sorry," she whispered, "but my time is due. Please go get Mollie Stover. Oh! It hurts so bad."

"It looks like I got here just in time, little sister. There is no time now to go for help." He saw the fear, concern, and embarrassment in her eyes. She started to rise and protest but could only call out in pain. "Don't worry," he said as he gently pushed her back down. "I've seen much worse than this. Easy now. I can handle it." He smiled, and though she relaxed enough to let him know she accepted his help, she averted her eyes so he could not see her shame.

The boys knew that their Uncle Isaac had delivered them, and far from being ashamed, they were intensely proud of their unusual birth and felt themselves as bonded to him as they were to their own father. Isaac stood, and with the two boys draped over him, one to the front and the other on his back, he staggered back into the small house. Once inside, their chattering and laughter subsided and they dropped to the floor.

"You boys go out to the chicken coop and get me some fresh eggs," their mother ordered as she wiped her hands on her apron. "We got company today, and I'll need at least a half-dozen more." She shooed them both out the way they had entered, with a wave of her hands.

"C'mon, See Right. I'll race you to the hen house," a high-pitched voice cried. And off they dashed.

"James, we've got some business to discuss," said Isaac as he hung his hat on the hook next to where the boys hung their moccasins. He turned back to face his brother-in-law. "Those cattle have been ordered and will be arriving shortly. You still have time to change your mind. Are you sure this is what you want to do?"

Isaac's brother-in-law sat at the table, his strong hands lay palms down before him. "Yes, I am. This land is better suited to cows than pigs or even sheep, and the money I can earn from them is better. If this is the way the white man is going, then this is the way I will go, too. This land may be 'Okla-humma', the land of the red people, but every month brings more and more white people. Abbie," he nodded in her direction, "works with me every day, as she should, in the fields, but it seems that little is earned from all our effort. The boys are energetic and help out where they can, but they are so young." He worked his square jaw for a moment before turning over his hands, almost, it seemed, in a plea, "I believe this is the way we should go. The McGarys have bought our old stock and we shall not look back."

He paused, and in the silence, Abbie placed two mugs of tea on the table. "Yakoke," said Isaac, "Thanks, Abbie." The two men sat silent for a moment, savoring the aroma of sassafras, hearing a distant rumble of thunder. "Don't get me wrong, James. I'm not trying to talk you out of it. I just want to be sure you really want this. I've ridden a lot of country, and I believe you are correct. This is the way to go. The railroad will soon be here, and then cattle will be even more profitable. I left those you bought to the two hired hands to drive in, and I rode ahead with your supplies. Listen, that should be them now. Let's go see." The two men rose and as James edged around the table, Isaac placed a reassuring hand on his brother-in-law's shoulder. They walked the few steps to the door and looked out to see the dim shapes of cattle emerge from a cloud of hoof-pounded dust. James said nothing, but his eyes shone with pride and hope.

The twins were on their way back from the hen house, each cradling his fragile cargo when they were likewise arrested by the spectacle. Two cowboys, both whipcord slim, whistling and shouting drove the small herd through the farmyard into the pen constructed for them. A single cow suddenly split off from the rest and tried to make a break for it. But as See Bird watched intently, one of the cowboys deftly, with a flick of his reins turned his horse, outflanked the bolting cow, and with a whistle and a wave of his hat, quickly reunited her with the herd. After the final cow had been driven in and the gate was swung shut, the same cowboy spun his horse and walked it past the two boys, still standing as they were, eggs in hands, staring in awe. He touched the brim of his hat in salute and smiled as he passed. At first See Bird thought the rider must be a white man, but then he realized the white pallor was merely trail dust covering that familiar profile. As he kicked his horse into a trot, the cowboy's long black hair danced in the sun. Both boys stood frozen to the spot. See Bird felt his whole body shiver with an excitement he had never felt before. That, he was certain, was what he would become. That was what he was destined to be.

Chapter 2

James McCarty was the boss of the Bar L, a fair sized spread that occupied pretty much all of the Pablito watershed. Yeah—the 'big auger,' he thought ruefully as he leaned on the porch railing of the big house and waved a pair of cowboys off to their work as they kicked their sorrels into a trot. He once was the owner of the Bar L, having worked his way up from cowboy to cattleman. The prior owner, Lloyd Smalley, had been generous to him with mavericks, and what with hard work, fortunate circumstances, and the love of Smalley's daughter, James, or Big Jim, as the men now called him, had eventually been able to buy the old man out and marry Leila Smalley.

Now, as he rolled his first cigarette of the day and felt the dry Texas wind on his weather-beaten face, he recalled ruefully how he himself had now been displaced as owner, not by another ambitious cowboy, but by a faceless association of banks and businessmen, mostly in Scotland, not a one of whom had ever experienced so much as a single day out here in cattle country. Still, it's my own fault, he thought. He dragged a match along the railing and cupped the spark. Two years ago a representative of the association had approached him and made an offer that was too good to refuse: In return for the sale of the Bar L at a price well above its current value, he would stay on as manager, run it as he always had, and earn a handsome salary as well. How could something so sweet come to taste so sour, he wondered?

Leila and his daughter Samantha were now "touring the continent." It seemed they did a lot of "touring" lately. Sammy, he used to call his daughter that, and he had really gotten into a row the last time she was home. She had been complaining about the ever-present dust and the stink of the hired hands. He had brushed her off, saying it was something a person got used to on a ranch. It would probably have ended there, but Leila had to jump in and say maybe they didn't have to get used to it, that he should give over the 'managering' business and they could move somewhere else, the east coast perhaps, or maybe even retire to Europe. That, he thought as he shielded his eyes against the Texas sun, was the straw that broke the camel's back. He got angry and said some things he wished he could take back, and now he was alone again in the big house.

Jim shrugged drawing his hand through his hair, graying at the temples. *Maybe Leila is right,* he thought. *Maybe I should just chuck this business. Times are changing. What with the railroad coming in next spring, the trail drive planned for this summer might very well be the last one ever. There had been a long drive every year for sixteen years. And he had led the drive for the first thirteen of them. Now he just "managed" the outfit, and Slocum actually "ran" it. Still, Ulysses Slocum was a good man, sensible and tough, and the men respected his horse sense.* Jim took a drag off his cigarette and considered his situation. *Well, if this is it,* he thought, *I'll be hanged if I go out whining and getting fatter every day. Slocum would be surprised, no doubt. And so will some of the boys.* Big Jim smiled to himself. Yes, indeed, he thought with some satisfaction. I'll lead this last drive myself. His decision made, Jim drew his wandering attention back to the tasks at hand. There are men to hire and cattle to round up. He pushed himself away from the railing squinting his eyes in the direction of a small black spot about a mile away. *What the devil,* he thought to himself, *if that isn't a man walking in.*

He ground out the cigarette butt, turned and stepped back into the house: He had always loved this place, its cool flagstone floor and the heavy log beams across the ceiling. He plucked his Stetson from the hook, brushed some imaginary dust from its brim and placed it squarely on his head. Juanna, the fat cook, who knew his likes better than anyone, silently handed him a cup of hot coffee. He nodded his thanks, took a tentative sip and stepped back outside. There was no doubt about it now. A slim man of average height, it seemed, was hiking up the long trail that led to the house. He was wearing a black slouch hat, fairly common in these parts, and was toting his saddle and war bag over a shoulder. Jim drank his coffee as he watched the stranger approach.

When he was about ten feet away, the cowboy carefully swung his saddle and gear to the ground and looking up at the man on the porch said, "Mr. McCarty, I was told back in Mingo," he turned his head slightly to point, "that you're hiring drovers. I want to work."

"That may be true, cowboy. We're about to start the roundup, a little later than usual, and I could use a good man or two. You got a name?" he asked as he drained the last of his coffee and set the cup down on the rail.

"Name's Carpenter, See Bird Carpenter," he replied.

"Indian, ain't you?" He raised one hand as if to silence an objection. "I ain't got nothing against the red man, you understand. They're some of the best riders I've ever known. And you say you can ride?"

"I've been riding all my life, Mr. McCarty. And I can do livery and blacksmith work as well. I made that saddle there."

Jim's eyes swung down to the saddle and roll lying at the young man's feet. It was well worn, for sure, but the rawhide working showed its maker to have a skilled hand. He rubbed his eyes to gain a few seconds to think about it. If this fellow worked out, it would save him the long ride into town today to find a man among the loafers who was to work . Still, hiring an Indian was not without its risks. Some of the men might get squirrelly about riding with one. That Apache cutthroat, Geronimo, was still running loose, murdering ranchers out in New Mexico. But this kid standing before him seemed respectful enough. Probably he had just drifted down from "The Nations."

McCarty was a man not to beat around the bush so he eyeballed the young man directly and got straight to the point. "Fact is I was going into town to hire a man today, if I could. You just might fill the bill. Here's the deal. I hate drunks and won't have one work for me, so if you like firewater just pick up your gear and clear out the way you came. And another thing. Nobody who rides for me wears a six shooter around here. I run a cattle business, not a gun fighting business. The boys play cards and drink. If there's a pistol lying around, somebody gets himself hurt or killed. But not here. Pay's a dollar-a-day plus room and board. That means there's a bunk for you in the bunkhouse and all the beans you can eat." McCarty smiled at the speech he had just delivered, and waited for the response. "Well, what do you say?"

"Mister McCarty," the young Indian replied, "that sounds fine to me. I don't drink and as for six shooters…" He raised his hands to show that the only thing hanging from his belt was a knife. "I got a Winchester in my roll there for hunting, and the pay sounds fine to me, too. You probably can tell," he smiled in return, "that I've been getting by on a bit less than a buck a day."

The young man's levity caught McCarty unawares. He barked a laugh and the tension dissipated. "Yeah, well then, you're hired." He took the one step down from the porch and reached out to shake hands. "But we should do something about that name. Some of the boys are likely to start hoo-rawing you about it. What say we just call you Red, since that's what you are, Red Carpenter. How's that sound to you?"

See Bird hesitated for just a second before he extended his hand. He liked his name. It was true his people often took white man's names, since most of them were Christian, but being forced into it didn't sit quite square with him. Still, it was a long walk back to Mingo, and he was hungry. That, plus the fact he discovered he sort of liked this new boss's directness helped decide the issue for him. "You got a deal, sir," he said and extended his hand in return.

"Good. Then it's done. After you get settled in, find Slocum. He's the foreman, probably down behind the stables. He'll put you to work. Chow's at noon." With that, McCarty turned and walked back into the ranch house, feeling pleased with himself. With this hand hired, he could get some of the paperwork done the association had been hounding him for. Although he was glad for the opportunity the day presented, a small part of him resented he had to bow and scrape to a bunch of paper-pushing city-slickers across the ocean who, so far as he could tell, were all sitting around studying to be half-wits. He sighed. *Yeah, well that's progress for you*, he thought, as he plopped down before the pile of papers on his desk. "Juanna," he called. But before he could say anything else, she was standing beside him, silently refilling his cup. "You know, without your coffee this outfit would probably just blow away. I know I wouldn't be worth a Confederate dollar. Thanks." She smiled to herself at his compliment.

After stowing his gear in the bunkhouse, the new hand headed to the corral, where he saw a small group of men working a horse. He approached the one who, with a leg propped up on the lowest fence rail, was issuing a string of directives to a cowboy struggling to throw a saddle on a half-wild mustang. He rubbed his salt-and-pepper handlebar mustache with the back of a knuckle. "Not that way, you danged saphead. Rafe, will you give him a hand? Luke's not used to riding anything but an old swayback plug." He shook his head dismissively. "The men I get stuck with!" he exclaimed. "I do believe he's plumb weak north of his ears." He heard the voice of the man who approached him before he turned and saw him.

"You Slocum?" the stranger asked.

"That depends," the foreman replied, irritated at the interruption and not taking his eyes from the scene before him, watching as the horse attempted to swing around and launch a swift kick at its two tormenters. "Who wants to know?" He turned and faced his questioner.

See Bird, also watching the melee unfold in the corral, took no offense. He extended his hand. "Name's Carpenter, Red Carpenter. The boss just hired me and said to find you, if you happen to be Slocum."

"Yeah, that's me." They shook hands peremptorily. The foreman cut short whatever he was about to say to See Bird and turned to the commotion behind him. "Luke, why don't you climb on out of there? You're just making matters worse." The horse he had been futilely pursuing was now worked into a state between panic and rage.

The would-be cowboy responded, "I almost had him there, boss." Nevertheless, toting his saddle, he beat a hasty retreat to the safety of the fence while Rafe tried to calm the beast down.

"Sorry for being so testy there, Red, but you see what I got to put up with. That's a good horse. It's one we just bought from Waggoner, down by Austin. But what does it matter if we buy the best danged horse in all Texas if we can't get a man mounted on him?" See Bird said nothing. Slocum's shoulders sagged a bit. "Sorry for unloading on you. We're hiring for the roundup." His eyes gave See Bird the once-over. "It's late this year and I guess we gotta take whatever waddy we can find." Then he noticed the handmade saddle draped over the lower rail by his foot. "I see you can work leather. Can you ride?"

Without saying another word, Red stooped and slipped between the rails into the corral, walking directly to Rafe. Taking the bridle in his hands, and cooing softly, he moved directly up to the nervous horse's muzzle. Within seconds he was stroking its forelock, still speaking softly. He turned his back to it and smiled over at the fence where the three men all stood watching. Spinning suddenly, he knotted his fist in the horse's mane and slid up and onto its back. Startled, the powerful sorrel dug its hooves into the dirt and rocketed forward, racing around the ring, seeking by sheer speed to dislodge the unwanted rider. But Red, now hatless, with knees hugging the sides of the steed, bent low over the flying mane, seeking, it seemed, to blend himself into the horse itself. His face wore a sublime expression of contentment, totally at odds with the chaos exploding beneath him.

When speed failed, the mustang attempted to scrape him off along the railing, but that was to no avail either. The rider just raised his outside leg and shifted his weight, lowering himself even more. Finally, the frustrated crossed-mustang broke to the center, crow-hopped several times and, then, seeming to lose heart for the fight with this relentlessly strong but gentle rider, came to a quivering halt near the center of the corral. Red leaned down over its mane until he seemed sprawled over the horse's neck. With one hand he scooped up the dangling bridle, and with the other he patted the powerful shoulder of the animal. Still speaking softly, Red flicked the reins and nudged gently with his heels. The horse hesitated for merely a split second before deciding it would comply and as peacefully as if it had been doing this for weeks, it walked over to where the other men were standing.

"He just wanted some respect, didn't you, boy?" Red said as he let go the mane and slid to the ground. He patted it affectionately as he walked it over to the fence, draping the bridle over the top rail. He turned and faced the muzzle of the still panting animal. Grabbing the bit with both hands, he locked his eyes with it, and still speaking as gently as one would to a small child, asked, "Didn't you, boy?" As if in response to the question, the horse bobbed his head vigorously up and down several times. Red moved closer and gave it a final hug around the neck. "We all do," he whispered.

"Well I never…" was all Rafe could manage.

Luke just hung his head in amazed embarrassment.

The foreman's lips, nearly hidden beneath the shrubbery on his upper lip, betrayed no emotion, but his eyes sparkled. His words carried the weight of judgment. "You can ride, cowboy. You can sure enough ride as fine as cream gravy."

Chapter 3

Slocum must have thought that See Bird, or Red as he was known around the ranch, was likely to be a good influence on Luke, because that was the way he called it when he announced who was riding with whom to round up the cattle for the long drive up the Chisholm Trail to Caldwell, Kansas. Luke, whose admiration for the quiet man who rode like he was born to it, bordered on hero-worship, whooped and grinned like the canary-eating cat. Red, as was his wont, said nothing. Luke caught up to him as he was picking out a couple horses down at the corral.

"Man, ain't that great!" he exclaimed. "I was hoping I'd get to ride with you. Ma wasn't sure I should hire on with Mr. McCarty. She said I should be in school. But Pa talked her into it. He said it was time I did something on my own, started earning my own way." He paused to catch his breath. "So here I am." His ear to ear grin was disarming.

Red looked directly at the young man. "How old are you, Luke?" he asked.

"Fifteen," he responded. "But I guess I'm most fully growed." He stood straighter. "At least I'm taller than you, Red."

"Luke," he scolded, "in case you hadn't noticed, most everybody here, except maybe the big boss himself, is taller than me. But I don't believe that a man's distance from his

top to the ground makes a mite of difference to a steer."
He softened his tone a bit, seeing Luke's freckled face flush
with embarrassment. "Now grab a couple horses, saddle
up and let's ride."

For several days, the two riders plodded north along
the ridge marking the westernmost edge of the Bar L spread.
Looking toward the sunset, Red studied the broad valley
that comprised the grazing land of Double Z, Big Jim's
neighbor. The two cowboys took their time, knowing that
other riders, like them, were also scouring the hills and
valleys, canyons and arroyos that made up the ranch. They
rode the high ground when they could, drifting the cattle
back down the valley, starting them back to the main herd.
The most difficult times came when they had to flush some
mossy backed steers out of the chaparral-infested gullies
and arroyos. Red was grateful for his chaps, for he knew
his legs would have been sliced to ribbons without them.
Even so, the work was difficult and dangerous.

The land was open here, much more so than back in
the Nations, Red thought to himself as he rode along the
ridgeline on the second evening. It was only down in the
small feeder valleys where they might find a stand of
cottonwoods along a small stream, that he sensed a kinship
with the land. Though his family's small operation was also
in open country, the hills and forests and rivers had never
been far away, just a day's ride to the north. Now that was
beautiful country, he thought. It was no wonder his people
had settled there when they had been evicted from their
lands east of the Mississippi. Someday, he thought, I would
like to go back there to those old lands he heard his parents

talk about. He cautiously walked his horse down toward one such small grove.

"Over there, Luke," he pointed. "There's a couple beeves standing around that corner where we can't see them, probably right in the stream."

His companion hesitated a moment. "Now what makes you so sure? I don't see or hear nothing, and we've been down in more than a few of these feeders, usually with nothing to show for all our efforts."

See Bird showed nothing of his feelings. Luke's observation was dead on the mark. There should have been more cattle along here than they were finding. Occasionally they had found traces of cattle, but often nothing else to go with them. Maybe the cattle had just wandered out and started back on their own. Maybe, but that assumption didn't sit just right with him. Still, he said nothing of his suspicions to his younger companion. Instead he said, in mock indignation, "Well then you ain't looking and you ain't smelling neither. That and the trash that just floated by tells me they heard us and walked into the water, probably to cross over. So why don't you just check it out. If I'm wrong I cook tonight. Meanwhile, this looks like a perfect spot to pitch camp." With that he dismounted as smoothly as if he hadn't just spent nearly ten hours in the saddle, and pulled a long drink on his canteen.

Luke knew enough about his pardner's skills than to show any more doubts. Leaving his spare horse with Red, he spurred his mount through the trees and around the bend. Several minutes later, hooting and hollering, he reappeared on his way back down the stream, driving about a dozen head before him along the other side, just as Red had predicted. He grinned and yelled as they passed across from the seated cowboy. "You're right again, partner. I'll be back to cook us up something special in a few minutes. You just make yourself comfortable."

Red chuckled to himself. He had to admit the kid wasn't too bad after all. Sure, he was rambunctious and talked enough to wear a man's ear off, but he seldom complained, and even though he was not a natural rider, he was learning and put in as long a day in the saddle as anybody else riding for McCarty.

Luke was as good as his word. It wasn't long before he galloped in. As he stepped carefully out of the stirrup he eyed the site Red had chosen for the night. Already the sun had disappeared behind the small ridge, and a breath of softer, cooler air crept through the cottonwoods.

"The horses are over there." Red pointed. "They couldn't wait all night for you to take care of them so I rubbed them down and watered them. You can feed and hobble them later. I don't think they're wanting to go anywheres right now." Luke eyed the small fire crackling to life before him. "I'm getting hungry, too," Red continued, "so I started it up for you." He looked up, his eyes twinkling. "You got any more questions? If not, then get to work."

"Yes sir, oh wise one." He rummaged through his pack. "What'll it be tonight? Beans and biscuits left over from this morning, or biscuits and beans?"

"I don't rightly care much, just so long as you make about a gallon of coffee. And just ease up a bit on the grounds. Yesterday your sludge was so thick I could of floated a colt in it. I couldn't talk for an hour; my mouth was so gummed up."

The two ate in silence. It wasn't easy for Luke, but he was learning to respect his partner's desire for quiet. Earlier, while collecting firewood, Red had stooped and picked up a small chunk of wood, examining it carefully. Now he retrieved it and turned it over in his hands several times. Then he slid his knife out of its sheath and sat before the fire, wood in one hand, knife in the other. Luke could restrain himself no longer.

"Now, what are you going to do with that, eat it?"

Red shrugged slightly and just stared at the wood, tapping it here and there with the knife blade. Finally he said, "I think there's a horse trapped in there, and right here by this little seam is its mouth. I think I'll just let the poor critter out."

Luke sighed and shook his head as if his companion had gone a bit loco and lay back before the little fire, his hands cupped behind his head resting on his saddle. "Red, this sure is the life, isn't it?" Though seemingly addressed to the man steadily working away at the small piece of wood, his question required no answer. Nor was one expected. "Here we are, free as birds, riding all day and sleeping under the stars. And to top it off, they're paying us good money to do it. It sure beats all the fussing at home. I don't know that I'll ever go back. What about your home? It must be great to be an Indian, living in a teepee, hunting buffalo, never having to go to school, and scalping people who mess with you. Man, I really envy you. If I…"

"If you don't shut up, you'll lose your tongue," See Bird exclaimed. The exasperated wood carver pointed his knife in the general direction of the stunned young cowboy. "In the first place, I never lived in a teepee. I lived in a house with my mother, father and brother. I've never seen a buffalo, and I've finished seven years of Presbyterian Mission School. You can't lump all Indians together any more than I can lump all whites together. Are you the same as the Germans, or the French, or even the Mexicans? Think about what you're saying. You are not stupid, Luke, so don't talk like it. Now I don't want to hear any more out of you tonight. You really got my back up." With that he resumed scraping and chipping away at his carving.

Later on, as Luke sat sulking over another cup of coffee, he would occasionally glance at his silent companion. However, unable to bear a grudge for long, and admiring Red as much as he did, it wasn't long before a new thought occurred to him. If everybody thought of Red as he had, then what insults and humiliations had this man beside him been forced to endure all his life? No wonder Red had become so angry. The more he thought about it, the clearer Red's position became. And the more ashamed of himself Luke felt. He threw out the dregs from his cup, rolled himself over in his blanket, backside to the dwindling fire, and muttered, "I'm really sorry, Red."

See Bird stopped his work and looked into the red orange glow of the dying embers. The intensity he had felt was gone now, replaced by a distant look of immense sadness, and then with a sigh and a wisp of a smile, "Me, too," he whispered.

Shortly after sunrise the next morning the two men were up and going about their camp chores. After a simple breakfast of bacon and biscuits, Red splashed out the coffee on the fire and ground out the last of the coals with his boot heel. They filled their canteens and wrapped the extra biscuits in their kerchiefs. That and some pemmican would be their lunch in the saddle. When they had mounted and climbed back up the little ridge above the campsite Red said, "From here we turn east," and pointed to his right. "In a couple miles we'll start swinging south again, back down the valley. Probably we'll see some of the other boys. We should make the ranch house by sundown tomorrow."

"That'll be fine with me," Luke said. "You're a good man, Red. Don't get me wrong. It's just that you're about as good talking-company as that stump you've been carving on with your Arkansas toothpick. And I am looking forward to some variation in my diet, if you get my drift." Red playfully slapped the haunch of Luke's mount, causing it to leap forward, nearly dislodging its unsteady rider—nearly, but not quite. *Last week, even three days ago,* Red thought, *Luke would have been lying in the dust. The boy is improving,* he admitted to himself. *Given time, the kid would be a good cowboy.* Luke shouted in triumph and kicked his horse into a trot. Red followed, smiling.

Chapter 4

The cowhands had been trickling in for two days now, and what had seemed like a sleepy cattle ranch had become a bustling beef station. On the nearby plains grazed some three thousand head of milling, bawling cattle. The south central Texas dust, pounded by twelve thousand hooves into a fine powder, hung in the air and clung to every available surface. Cowboys now no longer even pretended to keep clean, merely swiping their faces periodically with their neck-kerchiefs. Often, they could be seen driving a small group of wandering cattle back to the main herd, with their kerchiefs pulled up over their mouths and noses. Pens and corrals were being filled with calves to be branded before their trek north to the railhead.

Big Jim surveyed the organized chaos from the front porch of the 'big house.' He signaled his foreman over to where he stood. Tipping his Stetson back a bit, he snorted. "Is this the best we could do? Look at that rider." Slocum turned his eyes in the direction indicated, to see a young cowboy twirling in his saddle, holding on for dear life as his horse spun and he groped for his dropped reins. "It's almost embarrassing."

Slocum wore a grimace that could hardly be mistaken for a smile. "That's Little Bill. He's thirteen and is growed enough to be just between hay and grass. His folks are nesters from Arkansas. Settled on a patch of pretty worthless land down by Rimes. He wandered in the other day and seeing's how we're short-handed, I put him to work. I figure he can ride with the wranglers." They watched as the young man struggled to gather up his reins, losing his hat in the process. He stared down at it, lying in the dust, debating within himself if it would be worth the trouble to dismount and retrieve it. The two men on the porch watched as, with a resigned shrug of his shoulders, he stepped down from his jittery mount, nearly tangling his spurs in the stirrups. The horse danced a few steps sideways and Little Bill tumbled into the dust, landing on and crumpling his hat. "On the other hand," Slocum interjected, "maybe I should have him ride with Cookie."

"I don't blame you, Ulysses." Big Jim was the only one on the ranch who could get away with using the big man's first name. "We got to take what we can get now. The season's getting late and most of the real cowpunchers have already been hired out. We were lucky Red over there walked in. It appears to me we might well be the last outfit on the trail this year. We'd have been gone by now but I didn't get my marching orders from the owners 'til late. Hell of a way to run a ranch," he scoffed, "bankers from Scotland." Both men shook their heads. Slocum said nothing. He knew, from his long association with his boss there was something else stuck in his craw. Finally, in a voice lowered almost to a whisper, Jim said, "I'm riding along this time. The owners don't like the idea, but we're already short-handed." Slocum threw him a sidelong glance. "Besides that, I can read the writing on the wall. The trail drives are dying, and I want one more before I hang up my spurs. That's right. I'm seriously thinking about turning this spread over to someone else and heading on out to pasture." He eyed his foreman for a moment and placed a hand on his shoulder, "And I can't think of anyone I'd trust it with more than you. What would you say to that?"

Slocum stood straighter. "Jim," he tried to clear his voice, "we've ridden together since the start almost. I won't lie to you and say I've never thought about running this outfit. I most surely have. And that bunk house is a bit old by now. And I know you haven't rushed into this decision. You're a thoughtful man, always have been. The Good Book says there is a season under heaven for everything, so if you think this is the season for moving on, I can't stop you. Still, before I say anything on it one way or the other, let's you and me take this mob of horns and hooves north and see if afterwards you're still of the same mind. If the trail don't change your mind, then when we reach Caldwell you got a deal. Okay?" He turned and extended his right hand.

Jim took it in his. Slocum thought his boss's eyes might be watering up a bit, but probably it was all the dust in the air. "Deal," was all he said.

The initial excitement of the roundup had gradually subsided, and as the days wore on work settled into a familiar routine. Unruly calves, often weighing as much as 250 pounds, would have to be roped, thrown, branded and released, only to be followed apace by another of the same ilk. It was exhausting, dangerous, and tedious work as well.

One fresh morning following an all-night rain, rare but not unheard of for this time of year, a rain that miraculously turned the brown and yellow landscape into a thousand acres of green meadow, a stranger to See Bird rode in and dismounted at the big house. Luke confirmed to him that it was Joshua Randle, owner-operator of the Double Z. See Bird recalled culling out quite a few of that brand lately. He thought Big Jim looked a bit nervous as the two men greeted each other and then walked over to the bunkhouse, where the cowboys were gathered after breakfast.

Randle began. "Boys, I'm Josh Randle and most of you know me by the brand you've been running across. I'm here to tell you I appreciate all your hard work. Your boss and I have worked out an arrangement for the long drive. The Double Z will be leading the way and your outfit will follow north a few days later. We're heading to Caldwell and should be there by September, a little over two months. But, hell, you know all that. What I'm really here to say is that my boys are plumb wore out from all this cow work and asked me to challenge your outfit to a competition." Seeing the questioning looks directed his way, Randle turned to Big Jim. "Jim, maybe you'd better take it from here."

The boss of the Bar L nodded and took a step forward, hitching up his pants before beginning. "What Mr. Randle is trying to say is his mob of sugar-footers think they can ride and rope better than you boys. Now I've thrown in a thirty dollar prize to match his on each event that says you boys won't let me down. We need to break some broncs for the remuda anyhow. Show starts bright and early next Monday over at the Double Z. What do you say?"

The assembled cowboys considered the options. Nobody wanted to embarrass Big Jim. They were proud of riding for the Bar L. But being realists by nature, all they had to do was look around at one another to see the problem. While their best riders would stack up well with anybody, there just weren't nearly as many of them as Randle's outfit could muster. And even the best rider could be thrown in a few seconds from an unpredictable bronc. Still, there was that prize money.

Miguel Sanchez, a sleepy-eyed veteran of many years on the hard Texas range, spoke up. "Excuse me, senor Randle. Is it true you will match dollar for dollar?" On Randle's nod, he continued, "And all we have to do to win two month's wages is to do what we already do every day?" Another nod. Sanchez shifted his weight to the other foot, turned his head and eyed the silently attentive men behind him. "Well, how can we lose?" He held his hands out imploringly. "Even if we don't win, we'll still pull a day's wages. And if we do… Well..." As he turned back to face Randle and McCarty a slow grin spread across his broad face. "And besides, Senor McCarty, we've all seen the hombres that ride for the Double Z. They can't find their cows in a corral; much less drop a rope on them." He pivoted completely around to face the expectant faces of the Bar L riders. "Boys, let's show them what real cowboys and vaqueros can do. What do you say?"

The rest of the men, hearing this unexpected speech, erupted as though they had been fired from cannons. Hats were flung into the air filled with whistles and profanities as they jumped to their feet, swearing in righteous indignation over the fact that anyone working for another brand would dare challenge the Bar L to a test of skill. Even Little Billy and Lucas seemed offended by the idea.

Jim McCarty turned smiling to his guest and shook hands. "It looks," he said with some satisfaction, "like we've got ourselves a regular circus."

Chapter 5

By mid morning the following day, a dapper Jim McCarty wearing his best John B. Stetson and riding his favorite big grey, along with his foreman Ulysses Slocum, who had axle-greased his mustache for the occasion, led everyone from the Bar L, save Juanna and a scarecrow crew left to mind the herd, in a clinking, raucous parade past the front door of Josh Randle's big house. It was a comfortable enough looking log structure, See Bird thought to himself, shaded as it was by a stand of cottonwoods and pines. Josh Randle, along with his foreman Boadry, a serious looking man with a thin face and close-set eyes, stood on the porch and welcomed their guests. Big Jim's riders had driven ahead of them all the Double Z cattle they had identified, and on their return trip home planned to take all the Bar L stock Randle's crew had found in their roundup.

Every rider for the Bar L had put on a clean shirt and polished, or at least wiped the mud off his boots. Many had gone beyond the minimum to spruce themselves up. Red, in keeping with his new name, wore a scarlet kerchief around his neck and had strategically placed a colorful turkey feather in the band of his tall black hat. This impressive cowboy cavalcade made its way down to the Double Z corrals and holding pens, running a gauntlet of good-natured, and occasionally not so good natured, ribbing thrown their way by the Double Z cowboys.

"Hey there, little nanny, you come to watch the real men ride them big, old horses?" one taunted Little Bill.

"Now looky there, Clayton," his pal responded, "I do think our guests are looking a mite peaked. I heard they don't feed those poor boys much but cow chips and hay over at McCarty's."

After a few such comments Red could see by the way Luke sat the barbs were starting to get under his saddle. "Sit tight there, Luke," Red warned. "They're just funnin' with you." Luke nodded, settled back a bit, and kicked his mount past the pair. But a few steps further on stood three more cowboys, leaning on the fence.

They had a look and feel about them that made Red uneasy. Their unkempt appearance and slouches conveyed their disrespect, and as the shortest one turned to say something to one of the others, Red noticed a six shooter strapped to his waist. Clearly Josh Randle had some trouble hiring cowboys as well. These hard cases had separated themselves from Randle's other men and stared as Red and Luke approached. "I swear, Slate, I don't think I can ride against this bunch at all," declared the tallest of the three. "I got my pride and it 'pears to me they got a bunch of Mexican bean-eaters, mama's boys, and whoa... what have we here? Danged if it don't look like a heathen savage—a no good, ignorant, thieving, stinking, drunken Indian."

The third man, a large, shaggy-looking nondescript fellow said nothing, but spat a stream of tobacco juice in

Red's direction. He felt himself stiffening at their insults, but then Luke's calming voice nearby spoke up. "Easy does it, Red. I see their game. Don't play it. We'll take them later." Red smiled grimly and relaxed a bit in the saddle. Then, nudging his horse with his right leg, he sent it suddenly skittering sideways, threatening to pin the tormentors to the fence. Seeing 1,400 pounds of muscle and stone-hard hooves dancing their way, the trio abandoned all pretense of pride and scampered over the fence, sprawling in the dirt on the other side. The tall one called Buck, so gaunt he reminded See Bird of a cadaver, jumped up and slapped his hand down to his hip. But before he could draw, the shortest man gripped his forearm, restraining him.

Luke and Red whooped it up. Luke exulted, "Did you see those jack rabbits jump? I sure hope they can sit a horse better than they do a rail fence."

"I think you're wrong there, pardner. You're doing a disservice to the jack rabbits. The way they flew over the post looked more like pole cats to me." Laughing at the joke, the two Bar L riders urged their horses into a trot, leaving behind the three furious cowboys. Some distance away, the incident now nearly forgotten, the two Bar L riders pulled up before the arena created for the festivities.

Word of the challenge between the two ranches had spread throughout the neighborhood over the weekend, but the riders were still surprised to see so many buckboards and wagons from the surrounding spreads and from Mingo, too. A number of folks, they learned, rode all the way up from Rimes to watch. The big corral with its attached holding pens and chutes were lined with spectators, including more women than the cowboys expected. In the buckboards, pulled up against the fence, sat a scattering of females, most with parasols to protect them from the glare of the Texas sun, but just as many young women, dressed in riding jeans, boots, and hats, rode the fence rail just like the men. When the men of the Bar L rode up, a cheer rose from those assembled. Big Jim was widely known and respected. He acknowledged their cheers by doffing his Stetson.

One of the spectators opened a gate to allow them to ride into the arena, for such it had become. Not to be outdone by their guests, the cowboys of the Double Z mounted and quickly followed in parade. As all the riders walked their mounts slowly past the cheering, whistling, and waving spectators, an awestruck Luke leaned toward See Bird and asked in wonder, "Never in all my dreams… Where did all these people come from?"

See Bird smiled and replied as he tipped his feathered hat to a carrot-topped gal whistling from the top rail of the fence, "It's no secret. Those white folks breed like rabbits."

It was not long before the competition began in earnest. But before that, the prize money was announced for the three events; bronc busting, calf roping, and short distance racing. Everybody agreed Josh Randle and Big Jim McCarty were mighty fine men for staking such an amount, and the side betting along the fence rails and among the cowboys, competing or not, continued until the very moment a bronc would burst into the arena. Occasionally, someone would get a bit hot over some perceived insult and fists would fly, but such scuffles were quickly broken up as the competition proceeded.

Bronc busting was the first event. This was nothing new to the cowboys. Breaking in the half-wild mustangs was daily work on most ranches. And although many men tried their hand at it, the number who were actually gifted at the task was quite limited. And those few usually were rewarded with higher pay. It was a dangerous job that had to be done, as each working cowboy would use a number of horses each day, switching mounts as they would tire, so a fresh supply was always necessary.

Big Jim announced the rules for the competition from the back of his grey. "Okay, boys, listen up because I don't like to chew my cabbage twice. Each one who signed up, when your name is called, pick out a bronc from the corral. The wranglers will drive it into the chute, where you mount up. When you're ready, it will be released into the arena. You must keep one hand in the air at all times and continue to use the spur. Should you even so much as even slap the horse or grab the apple," here Jim rested his hand on the saddle-horn, "you will be disqualified. If you're thrown, you're disqualified. Ride the danged thing until it don't want to kick no more." Nodding to Randle and the man standing next to him, he continued, "Mister Randle and I will be judges. And I'm sure we'll always agree on the winner." He paused a few seconds to allow the derisive laughter to subside and then wrapped it up. "But just in case of a split vote, the good Parson Gibbs here from Mingo has agreed to be the tie breaker." The parson smiled, pleased to be incorporated into the program. "So, boys, the list of riders is posted on the gate. Get ready to mount up and let 'er rip!"

Never had anyone seen anything like this before, and as the morning wore on, there were the inevitable glitches. One Double Z rider, settling onto his bronc, wedged a boot heel into the fence and broke an ankle before he even had a chance to show what he could do. Another time, a Bar L rider, having selected what looked like an energetic pinto, found that when the chute was opened, instead of bursting into the arena, the horse hopped a few times, spun once, stopped, and looked over its shoulder at its rider in mild annoyance. Spurring only made it dance a bit, then stop. The crowd roared and the Double Z crew razzed the humiliated rider mercilessly. Experienced cowboys knew the pintos were notoriously poor horses.

When it was See Bird's turn, he walked slowly around the corral, studying the horses carefully before fixing on a mustang with an intelligent but mean glint to its eyes. From the way it moved among the other horses, See Bird could see it was a dominant stallion, and would put on a good show. "That's the one I want." He pointed. "That big fellow with the markings like a saddle that slipped to the left side. Yep. That's him." He watched approvingly as the wranglers cut out the horse, smoothly dropped a rope on him, and led him over to the chute.

Astride the mustang wedged in the chute, See Bird could feel each muscular quiver and shiver that told him this horse could not wait to show its unwanted rider who was the one in control. Then on the signal, the gate flew open. For the briefest moment the stallion hesitated, but it was only to gather its strength for a twisting leap into the air that ended in a stiff-legged landing, jarring See Bird's bones to his teeth. This leap in turn led to another which ended in a head down, rear up kick that nearly had the horse perpendicular and See Bird wondering if for the first time in his life, he had met his match. Shifting his weight forward, nearly standing in the stirrups, he fought to anticipate the movements of the maddened horse and to identify and match its broken rhythms. At first he had no time to think. He could only react from moment to moment and hope he would survive another two seconds.

When he successfully overcame the horse's first assault though, his confidence began to return, and his admiration for the beast below him began to blossom, for its incredible strength and courage, for its willpower that seemed unbendable. Just as See Bird would begin to recognize bucking patterns, the big horse would alter them. Several times the big horse nearly beat his rider. Once, in the middle of a sequence of leaping kicks, the stallion suddenly sunfished, and it was as much by good fortune as skill that See Bird did not end up in a crumpled pile in the dirt. It seemed as if this horse would never tire, that he would buck all morning and maybe all afternoon if he had a mind to. See Bird's ribs and spine were aching from the pounding, but then he slowly noticed a new sensation: He could hear the crowd along the fence cheering him on. Even the Double Z crew were lost in admiration for the skills the lithe cowboy was demonstrating. They knew this was how it should be done, how it was meant to be done, and how possibly they would never see it done again.

He found he was sensing the tiny muscle movements beneath him that preceded the explosive leaps, kicks and twists. Slowly, he began to more successfully match his moves to those of the powerful steed, until his pain disappeared, to be replaced by an adrenaline-powered ecstasy. He knew that no matter what the animal did, he would not be displaced from the saddle. Unable to contain himself any longer he let loose with a cry drawn deep from his people's past. It may have been a war cry. It may have been the sound a father would make on the birth of his first-born son. Wherever it came from, it was a cry of triumph, soaring from his soul. The crowd heard it and responded with roars of its own. The horse heard it as well. From that moment on, it seemed there was a change in the dynamics of power in the arena. Now it was the rider urging the horse on. The crowd could see that second by second, the man in the saddle was taking charge.

It was not as if the big stallion had lost heart. He was acknowledging, begrudgingly at first, the superiority of his rider's will. Once he came to a dead stop, snorting and panting but clearly as yet untamed. See Bird removed his hat with his free hand and reached down beneath the horse's belly and fanned it several times. Startled by this unexpected behavior, the brute erupted in a new series of leaps, to the delight of the crowd. See Bird had no time to replace his hat so he just waved it in salute to the cheering crowd, the horse giving its all, and to a life where such things were possible. As his horse was winding down into what See Bird sensed were its final leaps, he waved his hat at the man minding the gate, signaling him to open it up. As the gate swung open and the big horse saw the open plains before him, he ceased his bucking and shot forward like an arrow released from the bow. Bent low over his flying mane, See Bird whispered in his ear, "Fly, big fellow. Fly." Rider and horse disappeared in a pounding of hooves and a cloud of dust. The gate remained open as the awed assemblage turned to watch and to count themselves fortunate to have been here at the birth of a legend.

Chapter 6

"Red's Ride," as it was called, was the only unanimous decision made by the judges that morning. For nearly ten minutes he had matched himself with a horse that more resembled a force of nature than a mere animal. His "balanced ride" became the benchmark the other riders sought to match. And while none of them quite did, there were indeed a number of fine, entertaining rides by men of both ranches, rides which left the judges and the observers split. Had the good parson known what he was letting himself in for when he agreed to adjudicate ties, he most probably would not have smiled so smugly in the morning when his role had been announced.

Randle and McCarty, while good men, could hardly have been expected to remain impartial observers. After a half-dozen events, before a word would be spoken, they would sit and glare at each other across Parson Gibbs. The good man would listen in squirming misery as both men would state in emphatic and occasionally profane terms the cases for their favored rider, often at the same time. Then he would render his verdict. Whichever man was on the losing end would sputter and steam while the other crowed. But remarkably, both men refrained from making any charges which would cross that indefinable but unmistakable line which, once crossed, can never be retraced.

When Luke caught up with See Bird later around the chuck wagon he could barely contain his excitement. "Red, I got to tell you, I never seen nothing like your ride before in my whole life. Why, that bronc was mean enough to near buck your whiskers off. That is, if you had any. Not that you ain't a man. It's just that…"

See Bird found a spot of shade on the ground behind a parked wagon and settled down, careful not to spill his plate. "Luke, would you just cease your slobbering. I'm trying to hold down this flank of steak, and you're making it stick in my gorge. I didn't do nothing that any decent cowboy couldn't have done. You just got to remember a horse is a living creature that, with convincing, will let you ride on it. You want to teach it to want to work with you. And once it decides to do that, your job is as good as done. Then you let the horse do the thinking for the both of you. You eat your food now and let me eat mine." With that, See Bird set to his steak and beans with a vengeance. While "Cookie" over at the Bar L was a fine man with the vittles, he had to admit to himself the "Old Woman" working for the Double Z did not suffer much by comparison. He was aware of the fact the ranchers competed, not just with their riders, but for cooks also. For one of the best ways to hold a cowboy was to feed him well. Good cooks were in high demand. They knew it, and often carried on like prima donnas because of it.

The two cowboys sat, eating silently, lost in their own thoughts, when a harsh voice interrupted their daydreams. "Well, look who we have here, Turpin. If it ain't the little Indian and his wetnose pup." See Bird stabbed at a piece of steak and picked it up with the tip of his knife, without looking up.

"He shore don't look like much when he's not sitting up there on a big, old horse," the one called Slate added. Luke had stopped eating and sat grimly holding his plate with both hands. "And that's what it was, wasn't it? A big, OLD horse." And then, in the face of all evidence to the contrary he added, "And how'd you bribe that parson to swing the judges your way?"

Luke couldn't stay silent another second. "I don't recall seeing any of you gents riding nothing but dirt this morning. Maybe all you can ride is your big mouths."

Buck took a step toward the seated cowboy, when See Bird broke his silence. "Hold it right there, Mister. You better think hard on it before you make your play; whether you're meaner than the animals you got cornered." His eyes had become narrowed slits. "Cause if you ain't, you might just walk into something you can't walk out of."

Slate now became well aware of the big knife in the Indian's hand. "Easy, Buck. C'mon boys. There's too many folks around. We'll settle their hash later, when they won't be able to yell for help."

See Bird eyed Slate intently. "You do that, Slate, 'cause we're not going anywhere." Then he deliberately turned his attention to his still-seated companion. "How you like your steak, Luke?" he asked.

Taken aback by the question, Luke stared at See Bird and thought a second before replying, "It's good, real good." When he looked back up, the hard cases had taken the opportunity to make themselves scarce. "Red, I don't know how you did that, but I appreciate it. I guess I was about to eat some lead with my beans."

See Bird chewed a bit of steak and swallowed hard. "Luke, if you're going to live a long life, you're going to have to learn to think quick and talk slow. Now let's get these tins back to the Old Woman and head back down to the circus. Unless I'm mistaken you'll be up in just a bit for the race."

"I reckon you're right about that. I'm riding Diablo today." Luke had taken to that particular horse, a long legged black, and he rode it whenever he had the chance. It was a forgiving mount, and had shown immense patience with Luke as he learned the secrets of riding over the last month. Luke imagined it was affection on the horse's part, and returned the emotion. "I'll see you later." And strode off in the direction of the corrals.

See Bird, now with a little time on his hands, strolled over to where his saddlebags were stowed and, reaching in, withdrew a wooden object he had been working on in his spare time. What had originally been a small chunk of wood had become an almost completed carving, about six inches long, of a mustang rearing and pawing the air as if maybe defending his harem. Supported on a tripod composed of his tail and rear legs, he appeared to have thrown his head back as if sensing trouble to his left. See Bird turned it over in his hands, feeling the texture of the wood. Just a bit more fine work on the mane and it will be finished, he thought. What he would do with it, he hadn't decided. Maybe he'd sell it. Rafe had examined it and said that if Red hadn't any other offers, he'd like to buy it for two dollars to send to his sister's kids over by San Antonio.

Red had said he'd think about it. He stood a few steps back from the fence, sitting against the edge of a water trough, working the mane gently.

He noticed a young woman in denim and a gingham shirt, wearing a cowboy hat, working her way in his direction. It was the same woman who caught his eye as he first arrived. Now, as their eyes met she smiled. See Bird returned the favor and sheathed his knife. She was small but moved in a way that showed him all her parts were in good working order. Flamboyant red curls protruded from under the brim of her hat.

Without a trace of embarrassment she strode up and extended her right hand. "Howdy. I'm Mattie O'Meara. And I'm hoping I've got your name right—Red Carpenter?"

Red was both taken aback and attracted by her direct and open manner. He extended his hand in return, only to see her hazel eyes sparkling with laughter. Confused, he realized his right hand still held the little horse. Hastily transferring it to the other, he shook her hand. Her grip was surprisingly strong for so small a woman, he thought. His face must have shown what he was feeling for before he could say anything, she added, "I'm sorry for busting in on you like this, but I was on my way over for a cup of coffee and saw you here. I just wanted to tell you how much I admired your ride this morning." She paused a moment and licked her lips. "I'm mighty dry. You care to walk with me?"

"I'd be honored, Miss O'Meara. To tell the truth, I don't often get called out by a lady and I could use some Arbuckle's myself."

As they strolled over to the chuck wagon they talked. "In the first place just call me Mattie, because I wouldn't recognize myself if you called me, 'Miss O'Meara.' In the second place don't call me a lady. My folks own a small spread about six miles south of here. There's only my pa, my two brothers and myself to work it. So I've been riding and cutting out cattle since I was six. When I heard what they were fixing to do today up here I just couldn't let it pass. So when pa gave me the okay, I took off."

"I see. Well, Mattie, I hope you don't think I'm being too forward, but there's a lot of country between here and there. I'm kind of surprised your folks let you come alone."

"Like I said, Red, I've been riding since I was six. And I'm nearly seventeen now. And I do know the handle from the barrel of a gun." Then, sensing his discomfort, and seeing he had only been speaking out of his concern for her, she added in a softer tone, "But anyhow, Red, I picked up some neighbors on the way, so I have company. Thanks for worrying. Now, if you don't mind my asking— what are you carrying there?"

In an instant, Red knew what he would do with his carved horse. "Oh, this is just something I have been whittling on to pass the time." He handed it to her.

She turned it over in her hand and then lifted it into the light, slowly studying it from every direction. "This is really beautiful. I've never seen anything like it."

"I'm glad you like it, because I made it for you, even though I didn't know it when I started."

"Red, I can't." She started to hand it back.

"Yes, you can." He made no move to take it from her. "I've got no use for it. Besides, it ain't often a pretty girl asks me to walk with her. Mattie, I really want you to have it."

Darned if she didn't have a way of looking directly at a man as if she could read his soul. Red averted his eyes as if to prevent her from seeing what he was thinking. "All right, Red," she said. "I'm honored you're giving me this lovely wild horse. But don't you go getting all serious on me now. If you agree to dance the first and last dance with me tonight then we'll be even up. Is it a deal?" She reached out her hand to shake his. He looked at the carved horse sitting in it and they both laughed.

Over their coffees, she told him a bit of her Irish immigrant background and of her family's struggles to make it in Texas, after her dad finished working on the transcontinental railroad. Then See Bird shared a bit of his background, shying away from Oklahoma, preferring to talk instead about life on the Bar L. After an initial hesitancy, See Bird found her easy to talk with, but all too soon they had to go their separate ways, he to prepare for his next event, she to her buckboard where her friends Amy and Coogan Hanrahan were cheering on some hard-riding cowboy.

He watched her walk away, feeling adrift in all the emotions she had stirred up in him. It was obvious she was no wall flower. She was sure of herself. That much was for certain. She seemed to know everyone. And everyone she greeted was glad she had taken the time. It was just as obvious to him the attention she gave him was of like substance, friendly and open, with nothing more to it than that. There was no guile about her. But then he thought of the dance that would be held in the big barn that evening and of his holding her close and swirling around the floor with her on his arm. Things can change, he thought. Maybe things can change. But in the meantime there was the horse racing and the calf roping still to come.

By the time Red got in a position from where he could see the entire course, the race was nearly ready to start. Two barrels had been set up nearer to one end of the big arena, and the gates and a span of fence had been taken down on the opposite side to allow the horse and rider a longer track. A short distance beyond the big corral was another barrel, making the entire race course maybe three hundred yards or so. The riders would start off side by side. They had to round the far barrel and return from where they started. Only the fastest time of each pair would be kept. There would be no heats and no run offs. The best time won. See Bird watched the timer take up his position and signal the first pair of riders to prance their mounts to the starting line. The narrow-faced Segundo of the Double Z on a nondescript mount trotted up closely followed by Luke on the big black the boy favored so much. Leave it to Luke, See Bird thought, impatient as he was, to somehow work his way into the first pair. Still, See Bird had to confess the big black was a mighty fine looking creature with a barrel of a chest and legs longer than some horses are tall.

He thought idly about those horses. If a visitor should watch a cowboy working cattle, most of the time it would seem like slow work. The horse he rides may not look like much to some fancy Easterner. But See Bird knew that looks were quite deceiving in this case.

The good cow pony was a result of cross-breeding colonial quarter-mile race horses with the wild mustangs. The result was a horse with a gentle disposition, and an instinctual ability to work cows, cow sense, it was called. When called upon, it could produce incredible speed in the sprint. In some parts, they were already being called quarter-horses. He also knew that Jim McCarty was mighty proud of his horse flesh, having bought some of them from a W.T. Waggoner up by Fort Worth. One of the few times he had really seen Big Jim angry was when a drover came dragging in one evening on a mount as played out as he was and limping to boot. He tore into the cowhand, turning the air purple with profanities in his rage. After calling the unfortunate man nearly every insulting name he could think of he finished him off by adding, "I don't give a damn if you are worn to the bone. You can die for all I care. Cowboys are cheap. Horses are expensive. Remember that the next time you think about maybe working with a short string. But wherever that may be I guarantee it won't be here. I want you out of here by morning." Yes sir, Mister McCarty made absolutely no allowance for anyone who abused his animals.

See Bird appreciated that in his boss and figured it was one reason why he had taken a liking to the man. For if there was one thing that made the man from Oklahumma see red it was another man abusing an animal. On their small spread back home he and his brother had been taught by Uncle Isaac to care for all the creatures in their domain, horses especially. See Bird felt an affectionate kinship with the big creatures that could weigh three quarters of a ton, yet yield to a little boy's direction.

Knowing he could never outmuscle them, he studied them, learning their ways, heeding their nickers and the way they tossed their heads or moved their ears. He studied them until he believed he could communicate with them and they with him. And since horses are naturally honest—not like mules—he had grown up trusting what they told him. That was one reason why, except when he was forced to, such as in a circus like this, he wore no spurs. He told Luke once when the boy had noticed his spur-less boots, that if the only way to get a horse to obey was to rowel the creature, then he'd get a different horse. Of course he had never explained any of his thought processes about these things to Luke, but that was the way it was with him. He would not be cruel to an animal, and he could not abide someone who would.

Standing there, idly musing about things, he got to thinking. These ponies were so sure footed, if a man really wanted to show off how nimble-footed they were, he should take those barrels, add a few more, and arrange them so the horse would have to weave around them while it raced. Now that would be a show worth watching.

Just then the starter fired his pistol and the two riders exploded from the line. Luke's black was still digging its heels in as the smaller grey shot past. Red smiled to himself. There was no doubt about it. That man was a horseman who knew his horse. Luke's mount compensated for its rider's inexperience with its own strength, closing the gap to less than a length by the time the two rounded the barrel marking the far end of the course. See Bird admired the grey as it rounded the point. When properly worked, no horse could outturn a quarter horse. The smaller horse pivoted and swung its powerful rounded hind quarters as if it had been doing close order drill and rocketed back toward the arena, its rider lying low over its back. Meanwhile, elbows flapping, Luke brought the black around wider and aimed it for home. Watching the horses rounding the barrel, it was obvious to See Bird that Luke would not be taking home the racing prize. The grey streaked across, winning by two lengths, and See Bird did not see how anyone else was going to be able to run a more efficient race that day.

But the Double Z foreman wasn't quite through. He now brought the crowd to its feet with a bit of showmanship. After crossing the finishing line, the horse took no more than four strides before being reined to an abrupt halt before the judges. There it dropped its forequarters into a kneeling position, while the grinning foreman stood in the stirrups and tipped his hat to the judges and the crowd. It wouldn't affect his time, and he knew that if a later rider rode faster, well then that man deserved the prize. But he also was well aware it would be awhile before people stopped talking about his finish. Luke watched the show and smacked his hip with his hat. But his irrepressible grin showed unmistakably that he too appreciated the unexpected crowd-pleasing stunt.

For the next hour or so the riders took their turns rounding the barrel, and then the three judges put their heads together to compare notes. Compared to the arguments and disagreements they engaged in during the bucking bronc competition, within five minutes of the completion of the last race, Parson Gibbs stood and announced the winner. See Bird was not surprised that

Boadry, the showboating foreman of the Double Z, won the prize, and enthusiastically joined in the cheering and merriment.

Calf roping was to be the last event of the day. There was a delay while men from both ranches went to work reassembling the big arena. See Bird had to admit that Randle had a good idea in staging this hoo-rah. On the long drive coming up, with the Double Z herd maybe two day's ahead of the Bar L on the trail, the mutual trust and willingness to cooperate when necessary would become increasingly important. Riders from the Double Z would keep the Bar L informed as to what lay ahead, both the good and the bad, while the Bar L would be there for support should it be needed.

To prepare himself for the event and to work out some of the kinks he was still feeling from his morning's ride, See Bird wandered over to the big barn to work his lasso, or lariat as some of the men referred to the long stiff rope that usually hung from their saddles. A vital piece of work-a-day equipment, in the hands of a skilled drover the lariat could become a thing of beauty as it whirled and spun. Of an evening, many a cowboy would twirl it just for fun and relaxation, often working on crowd-pleasing rope tricks. While not as fancy as some, See Bird liked to work the rope and had become proficient in its use.

As he turned the corner around the structure he was surprised to see two other men, Double Z cowboys, with the same idea. Ropes were spinning and flying around, capturing nearly every time, some logs that had been set upright for the purpose. See Bird asked if he might have a try or two.

"Help yourself, mister," said one. "We're just about done here. I think we've roped those logs enough so that I figure if them calves will just stand perfectly still and face me, I think I might have a shot at that prize."

"No sir," See Bird replied. "I've seen some roping in my day, and it appears to me you boys are going to do alright." He shook out some of the stiff Manila hemp, building a loop.

"You say that like you're an old hand at this," said the other. "But the fact is you can't be near as old as us. Probably you're still a stripling."

See Bird laughed that easy laugh of his. "In years I guess you're dead on. I haven't seen twenty July Fourths yet, it's true. But my pa said when I was born I was holding onto the umbilical cord like it was a lariat, and before I could walk I'd lay on my back and lasso mice with ma's sewing thread."

"Lem, if I loved a liar, I think I'd hug this man to death. I'm called Quicksilver. Who are you anyway?" The three men shook hands all around.

"Name's Red Carpenter. I'll be trailing you boys north with the Bar L." He worked his rope loose and tossed a line at the log, watching as his throw hooked on top of the log but then slid off. "But if I want to keep my job, I better do better than that." The two Double Z cowboys laughed good-naturedly and were turning to leave when See Bird spoke again. "By the way, I may be out of place for asking, but would you boys tell me about a man that goes by the name of Slate, and his sidekicks, Buck and Turpin?"

"Whoa, Red," Lem responded. He removed his ten gallon hat and scratched his head. "A couple hard bitten cases if ever I seen 'em. Slate is the shortest one, but looks can be deceiving, if you get my drift. He's the brains of the outfit. If you know their names, you're already too close. They rode in a couple weeks back. Stick to themselves mostly. Said they heard we could use the help and they could ride." He shrugged as if that said it all.

His partner added, "Slate is mighty quick with the gun. I've seen him slap leather. Says he uses it to kill rattlesnakes. Buck is the tall drink of water." He looked at his companion. "I say again, he's a hot head. A couple nights ago the boys were playing a little five card stud and Harley called Buck out for dealing off the bottom. Maybe he did, maybe he didn't. But Buck went after him—like to kill that old boy. If you do tangle with him, watch out for his boots. He loves to use them once he gets you down. And Turpin don't say much, just does what Slate tells him. I'd stay away from them if I was you."

Red tossed the rope again, to see it this time snag and settle over the log. "That's my intention. I figure after today I'll never lay eyes on them again."

"Well, good luck to you, Red. We got to get a wiggle on. We'll see you later." With that the two rounded the corner and disappeared.

See Bird stood and played with the rope a minute lost in thought. Something about Slate and his sidekicks just didn't sit well. *Why,* he wondered, *would three such as them tie in with an outfit about to make the long drive? They didn't seem like the type to enjoy working twelve hour days, eating cow dust for the main course.* With a shrug, he chuckled to himself. *They may not like it, but they sure enough were about to start. Maybe that's what put a burr under their blankets. Leastways,* he thought, *he could be thankful they weren't working for the Bar L.* He shook out the rope, twirled it several times over his head, feeling the loop slowly widen, and let go, this time watching in satisfaction as the rope dropped perfectly over its target.

The calf-roping had already begun as See Bird leaned on the fence, looking at the cowponies milling about the corral. While the cowboy gets all the glory, he was well aware of the fact that without the right horse, the cowboy was nothing. Astride the right horse, the cowboy could do anything. Big Jim brought over a large number of horses to choose from, and the wranglers were cutting out the various choices for the competitors lining the fence. "Drop your rope over that one, no, not that one, the small chestnut next to him. That's right," he encouraged the wrangler. Kiamichi, he had taken to calling the horse he rode that first day at the Bar L. For all his spirit, the pony showed a keen intelligence and a desire to chase and work cows. With his short head, wide neck and barrel chest, he may have looked a bit odd, but See Bird had never teamed up with a horse so confident, so sure of itself, and with such stamina. *If I'm going to tackle a critter that is twice my weight,* he thought, *I want the best horse I can get on my side.* As the wrangler led Kiamichi over to be saddled, See Bird watched in admiration for a moment, then turned and walked to the chutes area. He failed to notice the lean figure who watched him peel himself away from the rail and likewise move off.

Kiamichi stood where the wrangler tied him up, saddled and ready to go to work. The excitement of the day seemed to have affected the cow pony. As See Bird stepped into the stirrup and swung into the saddle, he had to rein in the sidestepping animal to calm him down. When he felt the horse was steady, he nodded his head, signaling the starter to release the calf. As the calf reached the end of his string, the gate slammed opened for Kiamichi, and with a couple of crow hops he leaped into the arena and bolted after the calf. The lariat whistled over the onrushing cowboy's head. With the short "piggin string" clenched tightly in his teeth, See Bird released the lariat and dallied it gently over the calf's head. As the slack disappeared from the rope, he made a hitch and a couple quick turns over the saddle horn and leaped from Kiamichi's back. Without having been given a single verbal command, the pony was executing its part of the show flawlessly. Seeing See Bird racing down the line toward the struggling calf, Kiamichi dug in his heels and backed firmly, keeping the line taut. Only once, as See Bird approached the calf, did the line go momentarily slack before Kiamichi drew it snug again. See Bird flanked the calf, sweeping it off its feet with one arm, while with the other he quickly drew the "piggin string" around three of the upended animal's legs. He then returned to his mount and as he stepped back into the saddle, Kiamichi snorted and skittishly backed another step. "What's the matter, boy?" See Bird asked. "All this excitement getting to you? Easy there." He calmed the pony and moved him forward a few steps, allowing slack to form in the line. The judges counted off six seconds and then released the hog tied animal, which instantly bounded to its feet and shook itself like a wet dog before dancing off to a far corner of the arena.

See Bird knew he and Kiamichi had not embarrassed themselves. The applause and cheers from the rail confirmed it. Still, he knew they could have done better. After walking his mount back through the gate, before releasing him to the wranglers, he stepped down and inspected his horse thoroughly. Seeing nothing that could have been the cause of its unusual behavior, he uncinched the saddle and removed it, sliding it from the horse's back. "Whoa, boy. What's that?" His eye had caught something shiny as it fell to the dust beneath the horse. He stooped and retrieved the small metallic object. As he turned it over in his hand, he felt himself grow hot with anger. It was no wonder that Kiamichi had been so skittish. It was a miracle he had been able to function at all, much less show as well as he had. As he turned the star shaped rowel over in his hand, See Bird felt a knot form in his stomach. Someone had tampered with his mount. He knew that, from this moment, he would be backing down no more. He could take personal insults. He had all of his life. But his instinctive sense of fair play had been violated, and besides that, he could not abide someone who would deliberately hurt a trusting animal.

Chapter 7

Luke found him later, sitting in the shade of a cottonwood, a shapeless piece of wood in one hand, his knife in the other, working furiously to bring some form out from its chaos. "Hey, Red. Whatcha doin'? Working on another gift for the ladies?" When his friend didn't answer, Luke dropped into a squat. He immediately jumped back up. "Ouch!"

See Bird could not help but laugh at his friend's discomfiture. "Serves you right. Never squat on your spurs." But then the thought of what he had just said seemed to stir up other, less humorous thoughts and he resumed his carving with a vengeance. Luke, more carefully this time, sat beside his friend and watched in silence for a few moments.

"Red, if I didn't know you better, I'd say something's eating you up from the inside. But for the life of me I can't figure it out. You won a month's pay today, and if that Quicksilver fellow hadn't just beat your calf-roping time by two seconds, you would have won twice. Plus, you got that gal Mattie prancing around showing off what you made for her, just like she done went and won a prize herself. So it looks to me like you did pretty good for yourself here today. Now, do you mind telling me what's goin' on?"

See Bird looked at his companion directly for the first time, but his eyes still sparked like flint. "You're right,

Lucas. I should tell you what's going on because you just might get caught up in it, since you kind of threw in with me." He then quickly filled Luke in on Kiamichi's performance, his suspicions, and his discovery of the rowel that had been tucked under his saddle blanket. "One of the wranglers thought it odd that Buck had been hanging around the horses. I was just going to take my winnings and ride on back to the ranch tonight with some of the boys and skip that fandango they're planning. Now I feel that if I do that after what these snakes been doing to me, that I might just as well run up the white flag." Having reached a resolution, See Bird carefully tucked the knife back in its sheath. "I'm not gettin' run off. There might be some trouble, and if there is you should know why. If you want to ride on out, I wouldn't blame you none at all. A few of the boys are heading our cattle back home soon. You could help out."

Luke jumped to his feet and started pacing. "I appreciate your concern, Red, but you aren't chasing me off any more than they are. You're sure right about one thing, though. Those men are snakes. No, that's an insult to all snakes. They're lower than the belly of a snake in a wagon rut. I may not yet be sixteen, but pa says I'm near full grown. I expect I can take any of those fellows to the woodshed and tan their hide good. If we…"

See Bird interrupted, "That's just what we're not going to do. They expect us to walk up and start a ruckus. You're getting to be a fine cowboy, Luke, but I've seen you shoot. You're getting better, but it's a good thing you are ranching instead of hunting. If you pick a fight and they draw on you, you'll never see your sixteenth birthday. No sir. We're going to dance up a storm tonight, and maybe that'll put those three buzzards on notice."

The hot Texas sun had mercifully set, leaving behind a wash of crimson and orange clouds and a sky fading to purple. Soon that same sky would turn an incredible black. Already, a few of the earliest stars were making their appearance, as if they were scouting the way for the myriad that would soon stretch from horizon to horizon. Two fiddles and a banjo were striking up a lively air, and a few more buggies were just arriving as neighbors, done with their day's work, were looking forward to a rare night's opportunity to kick up their heels and have a good time.

Inside the barn, lanterns were being lit and placed strategically about the room. As See Bird and Luke stepped inside, the fiddle music seemed to double in volume and the air fairly crackled with electricity. About a dozen pair of dancers were stepping it off and sashaying around the floor. The men of the Double Z tended to group themselves on one side of the big room, while those of the Bar L tended toward the other. But there was no regularity or hostile intent to it. The men just naturally had a tendency to cluster around those they worked with every day.

He saw her and when their eyes met at the same time, See Bird could not help smiling. Mattie detached herself from her friends and walked across the floor to him. "Hello again. I've been looking for you. I hope you haven't forgotten you promised me the first dance." She looked at him so temptingly, it took a force of will on his part to refrain from sweeping her into his arms there on the spot.

"I don't reckon I could have forgotten that at all, Mattie. But it seems I've already been forced to break that promise. It appears the dance got started without me."

"Excuse me, Red," Luke spoke up, "but if you don't mind, I think I'll just pay a little visit to that big old punch bowl over there. But don't worry. I'll keep an eye out, like we said." He nodded his head and, tipping his hat to Mattie, made his way through the onlookers toward the refreshments.

"What was that all about? Lucas sounded kind of worried about something," she asked.

See Bird paused a second before replying, uncertain as to how much he should share with the curious girl. "Maybe something, maybe nothing. I'm not sure yet. But if we don't join in soon, this here dance will be over, and I will have missed the chance of a lifetime. Let's go." He took her hand and swirled her out onto the floor.

He took the lead and she followed as though they had been dancing together for years. Her rippling laughter pleased him more than any sound he could remember. Once, between dances he brought her a glass of punch. Thankfully, the boys had not spiked it. Most who wanted it had brought their own alcohol and out of respect for the ladies had not polluted the punch. She took the glass with one hand and brushed a wayward curl back from her face with the other. "Where did you learn to dance like that?" she asked. "Most of these boys don't know their right foot from their left. I'm like to be crippled from their stomping on my toes." She laughed and took a sip.

"My family, my people love to dance. I guess it's just in the blood," he stated as a matter of fact. "But it's no fun to dance alone. Mattie, will you join me?" He extended his hand.

Her glance was more of an appraisal this time. "Yes sir, Red. I'd love to dance with you," she giggled.

It did not take long for the women to notice there was at least one cowboy who could take a turn about the floor with at least as much skill as enthusiasm. See Bird found himself, as the evening wore on, to be a marked man. At least, that's how he felt. He once considered pretending to be clumsy to avoid a particularly plain-headed but persistent would-be partner but reconsidered and played the gentleman for her, at least for one dance. As the music came to a swirling stop and they parted, she was the one who thanked him, thoroughly embarrassing him for his less than kind thoughts.

Perhaps, he thought as he stepped outside to catch a breath of fresh air, he had alarmed Luke for nothing. All in all, the evening had gone well. There had been one minor dustup between two cowboys. Haymakers had been thrown, and one would have a keen shiner in a day or two, if See Bird were a judge of such things. But their friends stepped in and broke it up. The two combatants were later seen with their arms over each other's shoulders, walking like two half-drunken old friends. He caught glimpses of Slate and his crew a few times during the night, and he once locked eyes with Slate as he spun past with Mattie on his arm. But they disappeared and no one caused any trouble. Nor was there any indication they would. The thought caused him to relax a bit, and with his guard dropped he stepped outside and around the corner of the building to answer the call of nature.

He thought he heard a hiss of air before something solid collided painfully with the back of his neck. Stars flashed before his eyes as he fell forward helplessly, and when he tried to rise, managed only to come to all fours. The toe of a boot slammed into his ribs, knocking him over onto his back. "This is just a warning," a familiar voice whispered. "Stick to your stinking squaws, and leave our white women alone."

He rolled over and pushed himself staggering to his feet, struggling to clear his head. "What if she doesn't want to be left alone?" He backed up a few steps and then stood his ground, raising his fists to his still unseen assailants.

He heard a low chuckle and a gravelly voice, one he didn't recognize, slightly to his left. "Listen, you red nigger. You still gotta get home safe. She does too. You want to risk your life for a little piece like that?"

"Shut up, Turpin. You've been warned, nice-like, Injun. Don't make us play rough. Stay away from the O'Meara girl. She's ours."

See Bird stood, coiled, waiting for another attack, one that didn't come. He blinked hard but saw nothing. His two assailants had, as quickly as they had come, dissolved again back into the inky black shadows. When he was certain they had gone, he stumbled his way back around the building, gathering his strength as he went. The fiddles were quiet, but the banjo was playing some plaintive melody. The dance was reluctantly winding down, but See Bird knew for him the party was already over.

A few of the buggies had gone. As much fun as the day had been, everyone knew when the sun came up tomorrow there was work to be done, the same as every other day. Consequently, those with long rides over rough roads were already saying their thank-yous and goodnights to Randle and McCarty for staging such a grand party. Coogan had gone to fetch Mattie's buckboard, leaving the two girls chatting in the doorway of the barn.

"Mattie, can I talk to you privately for just a moment?" See Bird asked as he approached.

"Sure you can," Amy answered for her. "I have to say goodbye to a couple friends anyhow. I'll be right back, Mattie." With a sly smile she winked and turned to go back inside.

Mattie looked nervous. "Now look, Red, I know we had us a good time. I know I sure did. But I hope you don't think there's much more than that in it – than a good time, I mean. I like you and all but…"

"That's okay, Mattie. I understand perfectly. But I've got to tell you something. You say you can use a gun. Well, be sure to keep one handy on the way home. I don't think they'll try anything with the three of you, but I'm not sure."

Mattie ceased her fidgeting and her voice took on an anxious tone. "What are you talking about, Red? Give it to me straight." See Bird saw the alarm in her eyes, mingled with courage, and as the newly risen full moon bathed the night in its ghostly glow, washing out all but the brightest stars in its neighborhood, he took a deep breath and told her about his encounter with Slate and his henchmen. When he was done, she smiled at him, and standing on tiptoes, kissed his cheek. "It's very sweet of you to be so concerned for me. But don't worry. I'll be with friends, and now, thanks to you, I'll be on the alert. You just watch out for yourself. And thanks again for a perfectly lovely evening, cowboy." She took both his hands in hers and gave them a parting squeeze. "I think I could get used to you, if you get my drift. Here comes Coogan. Time to go. Goodnight." With that, the wagon pulled up, and See Bird handed Mattie up to the seat.

"Hurry up, sis," Coogan shouted. "It's past time we headed home." Amy clambered aboard before See Bird could be of any assistance to her. "Nice to meet you, Red," Coogan added. "My hat's off to you. That was a helluva ride, pardon my French. G'night now." With that and a flick of his wrists, the wagon started down the lane which turned onto the road leading toward the rising moon.

Chapter 8

See Bird and all the other Bar L riders who had not chosen to ride back to the ranch made themselves comfortable as best they could. Big Jim, as the guest of honor, slept in the 'big house.' The others were scattered about, throwing down their bedding wherever it struck their fancy. Sleeping under the stars on such a fine night as this was nothing out of the ordinary for riders such as those who rode for Jim McCarty. See Bird made himself a cozy nest in a pile of fresh hay out by the corrals, and for the longest time he lay there, arms crossed behind his head, trying to coax some sleep. Try as he might though, the excitement of the evening, dancing with Mattie, and the assault in the dark, kept repeating over and over. Something about it all, though, kept scratching at his mind and just would not let him rest. He pictured Mattie, Amy and Coogan walking their team home on such a moonlit night, chattering away. Surely the three of them, on alert, would be fine.

Suddenly he froze. Then he sat bolt upright. "I'll be hanged for a fool. It was right there staring me in the face and I missed it. I plumb missed it." He jumped to his feet and called out for Luke, hoping the young man would not be fast asleep and was nearby. 'Young man,' he thought wryly. Surely there were no more than three or four years separating the two. Still, it sometimes felt like a generation.

"Luke, darn your hide, where are you!" he hollered. "Get your lazy bones down here to the corral now!"

He was about to holler again and risk earning the wrath of all those bunked up in the vicinity when See Bird heard Luke's familiar if sleepy voice, coming from beneath a buckboard parked not far away. "I'm right here. Hold your horses." Without waiting, See Bird turned and walked toward the corrals. As Luke ran to catch up he asked, "Mind telling me what's going on?"

See Bird wasted no time stopping to explain but spoke over his shoulder as he approached the corral. "We don't have time for palaver now. Saddle your horse and I'll fill you in on the way. Mattie's in trouble and we've got to burn the breeze."

In a matter of minutes the two riders were on their way, galloping down the same road Coogan had taken what seemed now like hours ago. They didn't stop to give the horses a breather until they reached a small rise several miles from the Double Z ranch house. See Bird thanked his lucky stars for the full moon. The visibility it provided made it possible to run the horses harder than they would have dared otherwise. "Here's the thing, Luke," he said as they paused to look ahead. "When those two cowards attacked me at the dance, I didn't take what they said as seriously as I should have. They weren't just after me. They had something planned, and it involved Mattie."

"But Mattie's got company, and they all can shoot," Luke responded.

"That's what I figured. But I figured wrong. Unless I miss my guess, they'll be fine until Mattie drops off Coogan and Amy. After that," he paused, considering. "Let's ride.

We've still got a couple miles before we get to the Hanrahan's. Nothing's going to happen 'til after that." He kicked his horse into a mile-eating gallop. Luke fell in behind.

"Thanks so much for swinging by to pick us up, Mattie." Amy and Coogan were standing by the buckboard. Their father stood on the porch, a sleepy smile on his face. He heard the wagon pull in and stepped out to welcome home his children.

"Don't thank me," she answered. "It sure makes the time go by quicker when you've got someone to talk to. It's a long road, and sometimes it gets lonesome."

Coogan spoke affectionately, "Look, Mattie, it's very late. Why don't you come on in and sit down for a minute? Then I'll be happy to take you on the rest of the way."

"That's not necessary, Coogan Hanrahan, but thanks for the offer. I'll be just fine. By the time you two are in bed, I'll be parking my buggy. I should be going now. See you." And with that, she turned the buckboard back into the road and headed off into the night.

About a mile past the Hanrahan place, Mattie led the wagon down to cross a stream bed. While occasionally it ran knee deep, the weather had been so dry lately that at present it was little more than a trickle. She allowed the horse to pause and drink its fill while she took in the fragrance of the cool night air. An owl hooted off to the east in a small clump of cottonwoods. But nothing, not even a cricket disturbed the solitude of her immediate surroundings. For some indefinable reason, that bothered her. She looked around, feeling watched. She thought her mind might be playing games on her, but then she heard a twig snap. That was not her imagination.

The horse looked up from its drinking and flicked its ears directly forward. From out of the shadows and into the ghostly light, the form of a man materialized beside the road ahead. She felt the hairs on her arms prickle with fear as she reached for the revolver tucked under the seat. Then he spoke, in a voice, she thought, that sounded like it had been dragged over sharp rocks. "Now don't you be doing anything foolish there, Missy." He walked towards the buggy. *Where was that gun? It must have slid around during the ride. There it is*, she thought, as her hand closed in on the cold metal. She pulled it up and pointed it in the general direction of the shadowed voice. As she fired, she felt a hand yank at her, dragging her from the wagon. The startled horse bolted ahead until its halter was grabbed by the man who had first spoken to her. Now he spoke to the one who had dragged her from the seat and sent her sprawling in the dust of the road. "What was keeping you, Buck? She coulda killed me."

The new speaker stepped on her wrist, forcing her to release her grip on the pistol. She cried out in pain. "Oh, did I hurt you? I'm so sorry." The oily voice became hard edged. "But that's nothing to how bad we're going to hurt you before we're through with you. Behave yourself, and we just might let you live through the night. If you fight, well then, that will make it even more fun, won't it Turp? She heard the other man giggle obscenely as he dragged her to her feet and wrenched her arms tighter behind her back. She felt the bile rise in her throat. Oh God, she thought. Is this how it all ends? In the dirty road at the hands of these two foul creatures? For it would end here. Of that she was certain. There was no way these two would leave a living witness to the crimes they were about to commit. And since they were going to kill her anyway, she concluded, she would give them as little satisfaction as she could.

Red's keen hearing had picked up the distant sound of Mattie's pistol shot even as they approached the Hanrahan place. He had been hoping to give the horses a short breather here, but prompted by the gunfire, urged Kiamichi to run flat out. The valiant pony reached deep, tapping into resources it had never used before. Gliding through the night astride the pounding steed, See Bird knew Kiamichi would die before he quit. Nonetheless, he did not ease up, but urged him ever onward. Luke, on his big black, now fell farther behind but See Bird dared not slow his pace. What he and Luke would do when they arrived on the scene was another problem to consider. Luke was weaponless. See Bird carried only his knife and his model 73 Winchester short barrel in the saddle scabbard. Even so, he knew if he was too late, if those men had harmed Mattie, he would kill them with his bare hands.

If Buck and Turpin figured that Mattie would be easy pickings or beg for mercy, they were soon disabused of that notion. She fought as though her life depended on it, as she knew it did. Though Turpin outweighed her by at least fifty pounds, she broke his grip and turned on him, clawing, gouging and kicking so tenaciously it was all he could do to hold on to regain his grip on her. She broke loose again but stumbled in the creek, and as she scrabbled across the wet ground, her hand found a small rock. Turpin lunged for her, pinning her beneath his body. The smell of his sour sweat assaulted her nose, but before he could control her, she twisted around and lashed his face with the jagged stone. His giggling was instantly replaced by foul-breathed curses, and as he momentarily relaxed his grip, she resumed her struggle to escape, freeing herself partway from beneath his bulk. Suddenly she felt a cascade of pain such as she had never imagined existed. Unable to breathe, she felt certain her ribs had just been caved in. Towering above her and the cursing Turpin stood the second man. Even by moonlight, she could easily make out the high cheekbones and long jaw that gave him the appearance of death's head.

"Oh, does the little lady want to play rough? Well, I'll be happy to oblige." He bent down and wound a fist in her hair, yanking her to her feet. Turpin regained his feet and, panting like a winded dog, grabbed Mattie's arms from behind, locking them behind her back once more.

Buck surveyed her disheveled appearance intently for a moment before stepping forward, grasping her collar and ripping downward the front of her shirt, leaving its remnants in rags over her shoulders. With her arms pinned behind her, her heaving breasts were thrust forward, and there in the moonlight, half naked with her long red curls draped across her shoulders, Buck felt an unmistakable urge rising in him. This was how it should be, he thought. He had had a number of bar room floozies, but it was the memory of that girl he had raped in Louisiana that always seemed to arouse him the most. She had fought too, he remembered. And he strangled her when he was done, as he would do with this one. In his lust he stepped forward and ran his skeletal hands down her front. Her skin crawling, Mattie fought the urge to cry out. Instead she lashed out with a kick aimed for his groin. Her older brother had once told her that it was the surest way to disable a man. The spectral attacker barely anticipated her move and managed to turn slightly so that her kick only glanced painfully off his knee instead.

His pained grimace gave Mattie the satisfaction of knowing she had at least wiped that filthy smirk off his face before his open hand slammed the side of her face. "You really are a little hell cat, aren't you," he snarled, and then he back-handed her from the other side. "Turp, let's get her boots off first so she won't try that again. You won't, will you darling?"

Mattie's head rocked with pain. She could taste the sweet coppery flavor of blood in her mouth and knew she could not hold out much longer. Still, as he leaned in closer, she gathered herself together one more time and shot a mouthful of bloody spittle squarely onto Buck's face. From his baleful look she knew now he would certainly kill her first, before abusing her body. At least, she thought, she would have the satisfaction of dying before he violated her. His hands reached for her throat.

"Buck!" shouted a voice she recognized through the haze threatening to engulf her, "touch her and the next thing you feel will be lead ripping your guts out. Now turn around real slow!"

Mattie's tall assailant did as he was instructed, raising his hands to shoulder height and turning slowly around.

Then he coughed out what might have passed for a laugh. "Look at this, Turp. It appears like we got us two for the price of one. Slate was supposed to take care of him tonight when he was asleep, but I guess I'll get the privilege now. The dumb Indian rides in here like the cavalry and isn't even wearing a gun." His right hand dropped for the six shooter on his hip. It never reached its destination. See Bird, leaning forward slightly, dropped the reins and ripped the Winchester from its scabbard, levering off two hip shots in Buck's direction. The first smacked into his stomach, rocking him backwards. The second created a small dark hole in his forehead. Like a scarecrow with arms akimbo, Buck wobbled for a moment or two before toppling over. He was dead well before his head touched the earth.

When he saw what See Bird had done with the rifle, Turpin released Mattie and slowly backed away, his hands in the air. "You ain't gonna shoot me are you, mister? I'm unarmed. I never hurt the girl. It was all Slate's idea." He stared at his dead partner. "Damn! You sure killed Buck."

See Bird slid the Winchester back in its scabbard and dismounted. Mattie slumped to the ground. As he walked toward her, See Bird quickly removed his shirt and handed it to her. "Put this on, Mattie," he said softly. She reached up to take it with one hand, while covering her nakedness with the other. She saw in his eyes compassion and pity, where a few moments before she had been staring into the eyes of an unnamable evil. He looked so young and gentle. Shirtless, his smooth coppery chest made him appear almost boy-like and vulnerable. How could such decency stand against such evil? She wanted to warn him about the terror he was facing. But what could she say? Then he turned from her to the babbling outlaw. His eyes flashed like justice and his body seemed turned to granite. "Turpin, I have no doubt that you were in on this dirty deal from the start. And I know Texas men take poorly to scum like you who attack their womenfolk. But that's not my call. That's the laws', and I have every intention of turning you over to it so they can hang you proper. But first, I'm going to beat you hollow."

The desperate outlaw could scarcely believe his good fortune. A few moments ago he had nearly wet his pants in terror. Now here was this half-naked, unarmed boy, challenging him to a fist-fight. He may be the older, he thought, but he was also bigger and had picked up a few fighting tricks along the way. He lowered his arms to meet his attacker, but if he expected the young Indian to stop or say something that would give him an opening he was immediately disappointed. See Bird never slowed down a heartbeat, but with fists flying, strode directly within Turpin's reach, unleashing a barrage of rock solid punches to the other's midsection. The bigger man tried to retaliate, but his punches lacked force and seemed to have little effect on the young Indian pummeling him relentlessly. See Bird, having moved in on the other man, gave him no chance to use his superior size, but stayed low and drove Turpin steadily back, keeping him on his heels. The ferocious barrage to his body caused the would-be rapist to instinctively draw his arms in even tighter to protect his flabby torso.

But See Bird knew that one thing about trying to cover a part of the body in a fist-fight, which Turpin had forgotten over the years, was that a man who does so invariably leaves another part exposed. This was the case with Turpin, who as he tried desperately to protect his midsection, left his face unprotected, a mistake See Bird took immediate advantage of, sending a volley of jabs that connected alternately with the man's nose and mouth. Soon, a steady trickle of blood ran from both, and still See Bird came on, driving forward, pressing the attack, keeping Turpin off balance and unable to sustain any counter-attack of his own.

See Bird's energy seemed inexhaustible, fueled as it was by years of physical discipline and an adrenaline-powered rage. Turpin tried to parry another jab to his face, only to see his effort easily brushed aside and feel a powerful right cross slam into his cheek, cutting through the flesh to the bone. Years of neglect and wasteful living had sapped his body of its natural strength. He found his fists lacked force. He spat out two teeth before he finally realized that no trick he knew was going to save him, that he had, in fact, as much chance of stopping this enraged Indian as a calf would have stopping a freight train. This knowledge merely added fear to the punishment he was undergoing.

With certain defeat becoming more obvious by the moment, his will to fight back ebbed, and when See Bird delivered an uppercut to the chin, backed by all 140 of his pounds, the outlaw sagged to his knees, helpless and dazed, his jaw hanging loose. See Bird then delivered the coup de grace, a double blow to the sides of the man's head, crumpling him in a heap to the ground. He stood panting over him for a moment, then flexing both his aching hands, he said to no one in particular. "You'll live, at least long enough for them to hang you."

As the adrenaline drained from his system, he became aware of other sounds and sights now. Luke had arrived sometime during the fight and was tenderly dabbing Mattie's face with water from the stream, soothing the cuts and bruises that marred her face, with rags from her own shirt. He looked up as See Bird approached. "I would have helped you, but it looked like you were doing okay on your own. You beat that man into pulp, and he didn't lay a fist on you. Where did you learn to fight like that?"

"Back home my Unc…"

"Yeah, your Uncle Isaac again. Remind me, Red, if I ever get to visit your place, never to cross your Uncle Isaac." They both chuckled and even Mattie tried a painful smile. The two men helped her to her feet and up onto the seat of the buckboard. Red spoke. "I'm still worried about the lobo that sicced those two coyotes on us. He's still running around somewhere. Maybe he followed us. I don't think so, but I don't know for sure. In any case, we should make tracks away from here pronto. I am sure about that. We'll leave Buck where he lies. He deserves nothing better. If Slate does happen by, it'll be a good warning. If not," he shrugged, "by tomorrow night there won't be enough left to bury. Letting the critters eat his corpse is probably the best thing he ever did for the world. We've got to get Mattie home. You ride in the buckboard with her. But first help me throw that useless bag of guts in the back and take him along. I'll cover the rear. If there is to be any more trouble that's the direction it'll come from."

Luke nodded and turned to the battered young woman huddled on the buckboard seat. "You're going to be okay, Mattie," he said. "We'll have you home soon."

It was well after midnight and the moon was high in the sky when they pulled up to the O'Meara spread. Someone in the house must have been sleeping lightly, for Luke had scarcely drawn the wagon to a halt before a lantern shown in an upstairs window, followed by a man's face. "Mister O'Meara, please come down. Mattie's been hurt," Luke called. A few seconds later, the front door flew open and the man who had been at the window emerged.

"Mattie, Mattie, are you all right?" he asked as he helped her climb down from the seat. When she turned to face him, his jaw dropped. "Who did this to you, child? My God!" He turned his face to the upstairs window and called, "Mother, hurry down here right now. Your daughter needs you." He looked to Luke and for the first time noticed the shirtless young man still astride his horse, eyes scanning the deeply shadowed landscape. As her father helped Mattie toward the step onto the porch and into her mother's arms, who hustled her indoors, he asked Luke, "How did this happen, Lucas? What's going on here?"

"It was after the big dance, sir. Red here and I got suspicious of a couple no-goods and followed the wagon. After Coogan and Amy were dropped off, the two of them struck. Mattie was hurt, sir, but it looks like she put up a heck of a fight. We got there just in time. Red left one dead at the creek up the road."

Mister O'Meara cast an approving glance at the shirtless rider. "Good," he said, and then added grimly, "but you said there were two of them."

"That's right. The other one is in the back of the wagon. We're going to turn him over to the law down in Rimes in the morning, but we need to make sure he doesn't go anywhere before that."

John O'Meara had come to America to help build the transcontinental railroad, as had thousands of other Irishmen. When the work was done, he took his earnings and decided to carve a life for himself and his new family down in Texas. His hands were the size of hams, and as he looked at the beaten mess of a man cowering on the floor of the wagon, he flexed them involuntarily. "Robert and Seamus," he called his two sons to him. "Take a good look at this thing. It attacked your sister tonight, and only by the love of the Virgin Mary did it fail. Put it in bonds and make sure they are as tight as you can make them. Then cast this piece of filth into the root cellar and bar the door. Sit guard in shifts, never relaxing. If that door so much as creaks, or you hear any movement in there, I want you boys to open that door and make sure that it never moves again. Am I clear?" The big hands flexed one more time, and Turpin watched and listened in horror. Then Mattie's father turned back to Luke and Red. "You boys—I can never thank you enough. Your horses look spent. Robert and Seamus will take care of them. We've just got a small place so you'll have to bunk down in the barn, but that won't be so bad. Mother will bring you out some blankets and a clean shirt for you, Red. It's a clement night and the hay is soft. My boys and I will be vigilant. Sleep well. I will call you in the morning for breakfast. And God bless you both."

Confident everyone was now as safe as they could be, Red finally dismounted and allowed Kiamichi to be led away. As he and Luke settled down in their respective nests a few minutes later, Luke spoke. "There's just one thing on my mind, Red. I don't want to bug you but I gotta ask. I rode up there just as Buck and you were going for your guns. You were on a winded horse, going for a rifle hip-shot in the dark, without sighting it. But you planted two bullets in Buck's carcass, one in his guts, just like you said and the other between his eyes. Please don't tell me it was your Uncle Isaac that taught you to do that."

See Bird was silent for so long that Luke had about reconciled himself to the fact that he was not going to get a response. But then he heard See Bird's soft voice. "I don't know how that happened, Luke, honestly. Ever since I was a kid, there have been times when I know that something is about to happen, and a power sort of flows through my hands. I know I'm doing it, but I'm not the one running the show." He paused a moment as if collecting his thoughts. "I guess it's kind of like a piano player. He doesn't think about what his fingers are doing. He just lets them go. And if he's good, they do it right. My mother used to tell me it was God using my hands. But I don't know. Did He make me this way so I would kill that man? I'm not sure."

His voice fell silent, and Luke knew that would be all Red would say about the subject, tonight or ever. Whatever the source of Red's power, Luke knew he had been lucky to see it and luckier still to hear Red talk about it. "Thanks, Red," was all he said before they both fell soundly asleep.

Chapter 9

Though only two days more had elapsed before the pair of riders returned to the Bar L, it was clear that things on the ranch had changed dramatically. The pace of activity, now that the roundup was over and the long drive loomed, had slowed to a crawl, as though everyone and everything involved were gathering their strength for the ordeal that lay ahead. Final supplies were being laid in and the chuck wagon stocked full. The herd, officially counted and numbering 3,126 head, was fattening up under the watchful gaze of the Bar L riders in preparation for their long march north. The Double Z headed north the day before, and Josh Randle was still steamed about being shorthanded. Slate, Buck, and Turpin had not set particularly high standards as cowhands, but they had been counted on to help out. Now Slate had lit out for parts unknown, and the best Randle could hope for was to maybe hire on someone from some ranch they would pass heading north. And at this late date it was sure to cost him more. At least he didn't blame See Bird or Luke for his predicament. As he had told Jim McCarty, "If I had known what Slate and his crew were up to, I'd a killed them myself." And those who heard him and knew him, believed him.

Randle and McCarty worked it out so that the Bar L would follow close on the heels of the Double Z, using the same trail, or network of trails. Allowing for several days between the two outfits would leave plenty of range for both herds, and since cattle cover about ten to fifteen miles a day, that would put them only twenty to thirty miles apart, far enough to avoid confusion but close enough to support each other if need be.

Luke and Red noticed things around the Bar L had changed in another, more subtle way as well. When a rider from Mingo arrived at the ranch on the day following the dance, the telegram he carried, sent by the authorities in Rimes, explained the whereabouts of Big Jim's two missing riders in terse but clear terms. Word spread quickly among the Bar L drovers, it was obvious. And See Bird felt that, while they were as friendly as before, they seemed to give him more space somehow, perhaps more deference. Luke had grown in their estimation, as well. Or perhaps the events of the last several days had changed Luke and himself more than either of the two realized. He once caught a snatch of conversation between Rafe and Slocum, Rafe saying, "Yeah, the boy's fifteen going on twenty." Slocum just nodded, not smiling.

All the men knew the following day was the big day, the start of the 'long drive.' They were also all aware of the new rail tracks laid to Waco. Starting next spring, cattle would be hauled out of what had been, until recently a sleepy little cow town, by the thousands and then the tens of thousands. The cowboys spoke in quiet tones about what it all meant as they sat around in the evenings. It was a bitter-sweet time—the end of an era. That was for certain. But it also meant they would no longer have to spend four to six months at a time away from home. All in all, they decided in a sort of cowboy consensus, it didn't really matter what they thought. This was the modern world. And the old ways would just have to go the way of the buffalo. One thing for sure they all agreed on was that as long as people liked beef, there would be a need for the cowboy to ride herd.

"Alright now, men listen up here. I got your marching orders right from the big boss." Slocum stood on the rear of the buckboard he pulled up before the bunkhouse. The sight of their foreman driving the wagon was enough to get most of the men's attention immediately. "A lot of you men have done this before, but we got us some tyros as well, so I'm going to spell it out, but I'll only do it once. After this, I don't expect I'll have to reiterate myself again." At the use of this four syllable word, a subdued chorus of low whistles and 'oohs' emanated from the assemblage. Slocum smiled. He knew they were listening. "We're heading out before sunup tomorrow. We'll try to get in fifteen miles or so. The herd has to get trail-broke, and this being the great lone star state, and it being June, you know it's going to be hot as blazes. I'll be riding point with Red. The rest of you men flank either side of the herd. You'll all be switching off those who ride 'drag' so's everybody gets a chance to eat plenty of dust.

"Little Billy and Les will wrangle the remuda. I figure you'll each have nine horses, so keep them fresh, or there'll be hell to pay. I've seen men bake their horses and end up walking into Dodge. Another thing, boys, I know you are a talkin' crew, but working the trail herd, you're going to have to use Indian sign or something, because you got to communicate with the rider across the herd from you. And keep your eyes open." Slocum turned and pried open a large wooden case in the wagon. Then he turned back to the men. "Mister McCarty wants to be sure you're prepared, so I'm passing out pistols. Some of you are more useful with them than others, but there's nothing like gunshot to help turn a stampede. Also, we got word that some rustlers've been active up the trail. So every man take a six-shooter and plenty of ammo. But just don't go thinking because you're packing iron you're some Bill Hickock or Wyatt Earp. If one of you drovers shoots off his toe or something, it'll be your own tough luck."

Slocum paused after this speech. He could see the men were anxious to get to the Colts. So he held them for a moment longer. "We've got five hundred miles to go, as the crow flies. And in case you hadn't noticed, these cattle don't walk the way crows fly." The men chuckled in agreement. When it grew quiet again, he continued. "You men who have taken this little ride before, fill in those who haven't. This drive is what it's all about. If we don't get the herd to Kansas in good shape, then the Bar L suffers. This may seem like a big outfit to you, but I've seen bigger ones fold on a lost herd. One final thing." He could see the men were starting to get antsy. "This being probably the last time we'll ever do this, Big Jim himself is coming along. He'll be riding with Cookie ahead of the herd to pick campsites and noon stopovers. I'll be the trail boss. Now—no getting drunk tonight or all night card games. We got work to do tomorrow. So get some rest. That's all I got to say. Rafe, hand this equipment out. I've got a few more errands to do before we vamoose." With that, Slocum jumped down from the wagon and strode up to the big house.

The men pressed forward to receive their guns. See Bird hung back to the rear of the crowd. While life's needs had made him quite proficient with the rifle, he had found little occasion to use a pistol. When his turn came to pick up a gun belt and holster, he was chagrined to see only a right-handed set left. Being naturally left handed, his discomfort was merely underscored as he picked it up and strapped it on to check the fit. He sighed to himself and remembered what Uncle Isaac told him once about gun fighting, "It's better to be slow and accurate, then fast and dead." Well, he thought ruefully, if I see action with this I darned well better be accurate 'cause I sure won't be fast.

"Ulysses." Big Jim was leaning over a map laid out on the dining room table, tracing with a finger, the route they would follow. "We're going to follow the Double Z north just as we planned. They're already on the trail. We don't want to get too far behind, but we don't want to crowd them either. We'll cross the Colorado here, near Austin, and then on up to the Brazos. Normally we would cross the herd at Kimball's Bend, but this time we're going to take the whole shebang right through Waco. They built a grand bridge over the Brazos there, and I think it would be good for the boys and give the town something to remember—the last herd driven north to Kansas," he added wistfully. "Just make sure none of the boys jumps the 'reservation' in Waco. There'll be plenty of time for such Tom-foolery at trail's end. Then up here to the Trinity Ford in Fort Worth. I figure we've laid in enough supplies to get us that far. After that we'll resupply one last time when we hit the Red River—here." His finger stabbed at the paper. "Going through the Indian Nations is pretty much a straight shot. Trail's end is "The Border Queen," Caldwell, Kansas, just over the line. The Atchison-Topeka and the Santa Fe Railroad just ran an extension down there. That'll cut out the whole trek we used to make through Kansas up to Abilene."

He paused and looked up from the map. "My friend, I cannot tell you how much this means to me." He hesitated before proceeding. "It's time I told you. I've made up my mind and I'll not be coming back to the ranch after we sell the herd." He saw the surprised look on Slocum's face and continued, "I've contacted Leila and Sammy. They're glad and I can learn to live with it. I'll be taking the train out of Caldwell—just like an old bull going to the slaughter, and then on to the east. I plan to meet them in London and have already made arrangements with the owners of the Bar L for the orderly transfer of authority to you. It's the wonder of modern communication. How'd we ever get along without the telegraph? Anyhow, when you get back here, you'll be the head honcho and need a good Segundo. So choose carefully. Congratulations and good luck. I know you'll do well by me and the boys. We've ridden a long trail together, and it looks like we only got one more to go."

Neither of the two veterans were soft men. Soft men did not thrive on the hard Texas plains. Still, there was a silent moment before Slocum responded simply, "I'll do my best."

Big Jim nodded his head slightly, "I know you will. And that will be plenty."

Chapter 10

By the time the morning sun flamed above the horizon, the drovers of the Bar L had already put three miles between the front of the herd and the ranch. Had a spectator been able to observe a drive such as this from the air it would have been an impressive sight, indeed. Cookie, riding the chuck wagon pulled by four mules, along with the hoodlum wagon containing the men's bedrolls, accompanied by Big Jim, had already disappeared far to the fore. Next rode Slocum and Red, who led from the front of the herd, which was flanked by six riders to a side, whose job it was to make sure no cattle escaped and also to insure that any range cattle would not be accidentally swept up and absorbed into the Bar L herd. The head count had been exact, and it was expected when they got to Caldwell, barring unforeseen circumstances, they would come pretty close to the same number.

The herd had already strung itself out for about three-quarters of a mile, and as herds do, each animal had found its place in the marching hierarchy and would try to maintain it through the months to come as best it could. The natural leaders plodded forward with minimal encouragement from the drovers as if they knew right where they were going and intended to take everyone along with them. The rest of the herd followed.

Behind the two men riding drag came the wranglers with the remuda comprised of nearly one hundred and fifty horses. And the Bar L was trailing the Double Z, which itself was trailing countless other herds which made the same great drive, and plodded along the same trails until the earth itself had been reformed by this movement of men and beasts.

And while, to some, it may have seemed a picturesque or romantic enterprise, to the young men riding herd in the one hundred degree Texas blast furnace, the long drive was often tedium itself. Ten to twelve hours in the saddle, loafing along, not really driving the herd so much as following it, eating as much dust as beans—this was their job. And all for a pay day at some Kansas cow town followed by a night or two of drunken debauchery before heading back to the ranch once again, only to birth and brand and roundup yet another herd the following year. This is what the cowboy lived for, and by and large, he wouldn't have traded it for any other life he could imagine.

While the days may have scorched the earth, the nights on the Texas grasslands cooled so that, around the warmth of the fire, tired cowboys appreciated rolling a smoke, catching up on the day's events, occasionally spinning a tall tale, and evaluating the progress of the drive. To while away the time, See Bird found another piece of wood to work on, slowly finding the shape that remained hidden until he released it with the sharp tip and blade of his knife. Beyond the light cast by the fire rode the drovers on the first night watch shift. On such a night as this, depending on the drift of the wind, See Bird could catch the occasional sound of their gentle talking or quiet singing as they sought to calm their charges. For some unexplained reason, though they were being marched to their slaughter, the cattle found the sound of human voices reassuring. Yes sir, he thought, those cattle sure are funny creatures. While during the day the herd may stretch out for two miles or more, they would bunch together when they bedded down until the entire 3,126 of them would be contained in an area no larger than ten acres, often less. The blade of his knife worked the wood along a grained pattern. Maybe this carving would have a rider. It kind of looked like it might. His ears pricked up at the playfully earnest voice of Miguel Sanchez, the stout Mexican. Only Rafe, Luke and See Bird himself were left around the fire. The other men rolled out their blankets and were settling down under the stars as best they could. It appeared that only Luke was paying Sanchez any heed. The others sat with their eyes cast down, staring into and through the flickering flames.

"That's right, amigo," Sanchez was saying with a nod to Luke. "I've been a vaquero since before you were a twinkle in your father's eye. And I've worked some herds so much larger than this one they would be to this herd as this one would be to your own father's herd." He nodded in emphasis.

Luke just stared in awestruck amazement. "Is that for real?"

"I swear on my first dog's grave. One time, shortly after your War Between the States, I was working for an old ranchero down by the Rio Grande. It was one of the first drives, and we rounded up everything we could find to drive north. Almost nothing was branded, so whoever got the cattle, almost completely longhorns, to the rail head could make a fortune."

"Is that true, Rafe?" Luke asked.

Rafe just nodded, without looking up. "Yes sir. That is a natural fact." Luke turned his attention back to Miguel.

"Anyway, as I was saying, the herd stretched itself out so long that we needed twenty riders on each side. And they were so far apart we couldn't talk to each other for days. The farther north we traveled, the more range cattle joined in the parade until the front end of the herd lost contact with the rear. We left in the spring, right after the grass rose and the rains ended. So the front of the herd got plenty of water and grass. But the back end…" Here the portly Mexican shook his head sadly. "Maybe I should stop there." He made a movement as if to rise.

"Yes, maybe you should, Miguel," Rafe said.

"You can't just stop there." Luke's voice was pleading. "What happened?"

Miguel sighed as if in resignation and sat back down. "Well, since you insist. When we got to Abilene, the front of the herd started bedding down as usual while the rest of the herd kept coming up. They came up that night and all the next day, looking scragglier and scragglier. That second night, the stragglers started walking right over those already bedded down, causing such a ruckus as you could only imagine. They wouldn't turn for man, horse or cow. We had our hands full trying to calm them all down. When one walked into the side of my horse as if it wasn't there, I finally caught on to what was happening. The poor creatures were completely blind."

"Now just a minute," Luke started to rise.

"No, by Moses and the rock, I swear it's true. What happened was the herd was so large the front end of it drunk up all the water in the streams we crossed, leaving nothing for those at the rear. That's right, amigo. The herd was so big those in the front were well watered while those in the rear were blind with thirst."

With the cessation of the narrative, Luke looked around the fire to check the reactions of the others. See Bird, as usual, said nothing. Finally Rafe slapped his knees and guffawed. "If you don't just take the cake, Lucas. That old liar fed you last year's bacon and you thought it was steak."

Luke eyed Sanchez, unsure of what to say or do. The story teller just stared back, looking offended. "Every word I told you was the truth, I swear."

"Sure you do," Rafe added, "on your first dog's grave." He burst into laughter again. Luke's face softened into a smile that spread across his freckles. Even See Bird stabbed his knife into the ground and silently shook his shoulders, joining in the merriment.

Luke started to turn away in mock disgust. "Wait, amigo," Miguel said. "Have I told you about my first dog?"

"You mean the one you et?" Rafe asked. And this time even See Bird joined in the laughter.

A few mornings later, just as the Bar L drovers were about to set the herd in motion again, See Bird was surprised to see Big Jim with Slocum, both mounted, talking animatedly and pointing off to the northeast from atop a small knob. In a minute Slocum rode down and Big Jim disappeared down the other side.

"Okay, men, gather round and spread the word." Slocum clearly was not entirely pleased with what he was about to say. "The boss has decided since this is the last long drive for the Bar L or maybe for anybody else as well, we're going to have a little parade. Normally, we would follow the Double Z around to the northwest and ford the Brazos. But the kind folks in Waco have built this lovely bridge and the boss is bound and determined for us to use it. Now I've got nothing against using a bridge, but I've got to warn you drovers. Keep a close watch on the herd. Bunch them up tight as you can and force them through and on out of town. We are not stopping. You got that?"

"Why sure, boss. But what's the problem?" spoke a voice from the rear.

Slocum took a deep breath. "It's really not the herd I'm worried about. It's you boys. Some of you youngsters might not be aware of it, but you veterans will know what I am talking about. The good folks of Waco, in their wisdom, have set up a section of town called the Reservation. All I'll say is that respectable citizens do not dally there. Any of you boys who neglect your duty for even ten minutes will be immediately fired. You'll have plenty of time for such shenanigans on the return ride. Am I clear, or do I need to spell it out?"

A cowboy next to See Bird muttered under his breath, "If I could find me a dolly, I guarantee it wouldn't take me no ten minutes." He sniggered and the men turned to their horses.

Chapter 11

Jim McCarty rode into Waco ahead of the herd. He had some personal business to attend to. Riding down the main street, he felt as though he scarcely recognized the town. With the railroad coming in, Waco was bustling and bursting at the seams. On a corner where he remembered a false-front two story wooden saloon now stood an impressive four story brick bank guarded by two tall white pillars. The air seemed filled with the music of hammers pounding nails and the metallic clinking of wagon gear. Finally, he pulled his horse up in front of a familiar building and hitched it to the rail. "Amos," he yelled as he mounted the boardwalk. "You old coot. Where are you?" he called as he strode through the open door.

"Well, dog my cats, if it ain't Jim McCarty." A heavy-set balding man in an apron stepped around the counter, a pair of frameless glasses perched precariously on the tip of his bulbous nose. "What brings you to town?"

"Amos, you old snake oil salesman." Jim's warm smile and firm handshake belied his words. "I'm hauling my outfit up to Kansas and thought I would stop in for a minute. They're right behind so I've gotta run. I was just hoping…" Jim rubbed his stomach, "I was just hoping maybe you'd have something amongst your concoctions for a gut ache that's been putting a hitch in my giddy-up for a few days now. I believe Cookie must have tossed something special in the beans and I can't seem to shake it, if you get my drift."

Amos removed his glasses and sucked on the ear wire. "Now Jim, if you're not putting me on, I may have just what the doctor ordered. You know I love to experiment." His pale blue eyes twinkled. "This time I think I really have something." He went behind the counter and emerged with a jug from which he poured out an amber colored beverage. Try this and tell me what you think.

Hesitantly, Big Jim reached down and picked up the glass, waving it beneath his nose. "Smells okay," he said. "Well, it can't do me any more harm than what Cookie already has. Bottoms up." With that he took a large gulp and set the glass down. "That ain't half bad," he added approvingly and then drained the rest. "Matter of fact, I like it tolerably well. What is it?"

"I know what's in it," Amos rejoined. "Almost everything I can think of. I'm just not sure what to call it. I've been referring to it as my Pepper-Upper. What do you think?"

Big Jim looked thoughtful. "Pepper-Upper might do, but it sounds a mite childish. We're talking about something medicinal here as well."

"You're right, Jim." He snapped his fingers. "Holy cow, man, you just gave it to me. Excuse me but I've got to get back to work. Yes, that's it," he replied, obviously preoccupied with his thoughts. He started hustling away to a back room, carefully cradling the jug with the remaining liquid, leaving Jim entirely forgotten.

"Well, what are you going to call it then?" he asked.

"Oh yes. Forgive me, Jim. I'm going to call it Doctor Pepper."

"Doctor Pepper," Jim repeated as he walked back down to his horse. "I don't know." He remounted and noticed his stomach seemed to have settled down a bit. As he turned his horse and started back down the dusty street, half clogged with buggies and pedestrians, he thought about Amos. "Foolish dreamer. Doctor Pepper. What a silly name. It'll never catch on. Oh well, that's not my problem. He-ah, let's go boy." He kicked his mount into a gallop and disappeared around a corner.

The march of the Bar L through Waco was a resounding success. Other than for three cows that managed briefly to break free for a quick romp through Millie's Millinery, the entire herd, flanked by sixteen whistling, hat waving cowboys, made the trek through town without incident, except perhaps, when it passed the corner of Osage and Buffalo Street, where a clutch of 'painted ladies of the line,' fresh off the Reservation, did their best to lure some cowboys astray, all to no avail. Slocum's warning and their empty wallets ensured their good behavior. Before nightfall the entire herd was some twelve miles north of town, bedded down as peaceably as though they had never seen Waco, Texas.

Chapter 12

Ten days and nearly a hundred and fifty hard miles later, See Bird and Slocum slouched in their saddles and unwrapped the biscuits they saved from breakfast. Having just changed horses they decided this would be as good a time as any for a noon break—sinkers washed down by warm water from their canteens. This was all they would eat until evening. But it didn't bother them much because it was what they did almost every day. And the evening meals more than made up for it. Last night's meal was typical. Cookie prepared stewed beef, plenty of beans and sinkers and topped it off with those sweet and juicy canned peaches. The whole meal was washed down with buckets of thick black coffee. Both riders knew there would be more of the same tonight. *Cookie may be an irascible old grouch,* See Bird thought, and he may have been pulling down a considerably larger pay than was the drover, but See Bird knew that should something happen to him, it would be an inconvenience for awhile until a new hand could be hired, but if the Bar L lost Cookie it would be a disaster of the first magnitude.

The two observed the herd resting below in a long, green, shallow valley by a small stream. They were lucky, Slocum thought, to find water still coursing here. The land had been dry the last few days. Two days without water had the herd growing restless. So when they came upon the small stream, even though it was still technically morning, he decided to halt the herd and let them rest up a bit. They could start up again a bit later, after the worst heat of the day, and travel a little longer into the evening. It would not do to bring the herd into Caldwell gaunt and trail beaten. The plan was to fatten them up as they walked, not wear them out to hide and bone.

Both men glanced to the north, seeing a low brown smudge hanging just above the horizon. "Looks like we're right on the Double Z's tail, Red," Slocum said, taking another bite. "They can't be more than twelve, maybe fifteen miles ahead, I figure."

"Just so," See Bird concurred.

"Red, I didn't get this job by ignoring what's important. And I get the feeling that you've been chewing something over for the past few days. You're working harder and harder on your whittling, and talking even less than usual. Is there something I oughta know?" He spoke without ever taking his eyes from the horizon.

See Bird paused a few moments to collect his thoughts. "Maybe there is," he finally spoke. "A few things have been aggravating my mind lately that I can't seem to puzzle out on my own. And it all runs around Slate."

Slocum nodded as if what See Bird said had struck a responsive chord in him as well. The young Indian continued. "When Luke and me were riding the line during roundup there were a number of times I saw some trace of cattle, maybe two weeks or more old, but no stock to account for it. Maybe they had drifted on down on their own, I thought. But I'm not sure. I just got the feeling there should have been more of them. Maybe they wandered over onto the Double Z range, but then we didn't get nearly that many of ours back from them when we exchanged. Now two of Slate's gang are gone, and he's disappeared. Were Buck and Turp his only men? I don't mean to sound suspicious, but what do you know of that crew we're trailing?"

"Red, I don't rightly know what to make of it all. I've given a lot of thought to the same question, even talked with Big Jim about it. I think Randle is a straight shooter. True, he tends to strut around like a Bandy Rooster, but I've known him for a long time, and I think he's okay. But he ain't along on this trip. His foreman Boadry is the trail boss and he's cut from a different bolt of cloth." Slocum hesitated and then continued. "I guess I'd ride with him, too. He's good with cattle and horses but maybe not too terribly bright when it comes to reading men. He's always played straight with me, so I think he just got suckered into some bad hires. And if that's true, there may well be another rotten apple in their barrel."

"That's about the way I read it," See Bird answered. "I was hoping you did, too. But that just brings me up against a brick wall. What was Slate's angle? He and his crew sure didn't hire on because they wanted to work. And I can't believe it was just to cut out a few of our cattle at roundup."

Slocum smiled to himself at Red's use of the word 'our.' It proved what had already become obvious: The man could be counted on to back the brand if push should ever come to shove. "There's a lot of things we can't control—the weather, rivers, rattlers and rustlers are just a few. But we can be alert and handle them as best we can should the need arise. We're close enough to be in contact with the Double Z. If they run into anything, we'll know shortly enough." He eyed his companion directly. "So keep your eyes open and your Winchester loaded."

Red nodded his assent.

By the next morning the weather had taken a turn so the entire countryside seemed cloaked in a grey, hazy mist. With the sun blotted out, north was anyone's guess. Still, the herd plodded on. The men broke out their 'fish,' as they called their slickers; to keep from being soaked in the off-and-on again showers. But it didn't make them any happier. Being hot and uncomfortable inside their long coats was little solace for remaining dry, and the mood of the drovers changed from resigned to sullen. They had been trail riding for nearly a month and they were still days away from the Red River.

The following morning saw the weather deteriorate even more. Sheets of swirling rain whipped against them from all sides, sending small rivulets down the backs of the long coats. The men became soaked through, and though they tried to stay as dry as possible, even the fire in the evening seemed insufficient to dry their soggy things. The third wet day started out as had the previous two. Still the herd continued its relentless trek. By evening, though the rain system seemed to have spent most of its energy and was winding down to fits of drizzle, Sanchez remarked as to how he couldn't remember a time when he wasn't wet. Still the night watch rode its unceasing rounds about the bedded-down herd, singing and talking to the restless beeves.

Tempers grew short, and comments that ordinarily would have drawn no response or a shrug and a laugh now set men on edge. See Bird heard Rafe laying into Little Billy one evening for not properly caring for the remuda, nearly driving the young man to tears. And while See Bird could understand Rafe's desire to impress upon the young man the necessity of keeping the horse herd in top condition, he could sympathize with Little Billy and the difficult conditions the boy had to work under.

They were all huddled around the fire drinking hot coffee, watching the rain drip from the brims of their hats when the thud of approaching hooves announced the arrival of a visitor. It was Clayton, a drover for the Double Z, who stepped down from his horse and into the firelight. Big Jim stood to greet him.

"Howdy there, Clayton. Looks like you're a long way from your outfit. Did you get lost or something?"

Clayton chuckled, "No, nothing like that, Mister McCarty. But what ol' Dan'l Boone once said does come to mind. When he was asked if he'd ever been lost, he thought about it a second and then said, 'No, but I was bewildered once for three days.' I know what he felt like. I'm here because the boss just got a wire delivered today from up at Dendy's. He thought you might like know about it. It concerns that fellow your man Red turned over to the law down in Rimes."

"Yes sir. I sure would like to hear about that. But it looks like you've been riding hard on short rations. Little Billy, take care of his horse, would you? And Clayton, you just head over to the chuck wagon and fill up a plate for yourself. We'll talk after you've fed and caught your breath a bit."

"Thank you kindly, Mister McCarty. My horse and I are about done in. I gotta admit it was a bit tricky finding your fire in this mess, but I'll take you up on your offer and be right back." With that Clayton walked over to the chuck wagon where Cookie was working away under a stretched canvas awning. He made it a point to make his most benevolent impression on the tired cowboy, ladling up the best of the meat from the bottom of the stew pot.

News of the visitor traveled fast, and by the time Clayton was finished sopping up the gravy with a biscuit and licking his fingers clean, he was aware that probably everyone who was not working a shift was sitting around that fire with their eyes glued on him, all wanting to know how the business with Turp had turned out. "Thanks, Cookie," he yelled over his shoulder. "That was a mighty fine feast. Food that tastes so good as that could cause a man to leave his home for it." Cookie smiled back and saluted with a spatula. "And now, Mister McCarty, I better get down to business and say what I come to tell you." Everybody seemed to lean in to hear better. "Turp is executed. That's for sure." Clayton interspersed his pronouncements with bites of dried apples. "He was hung after a fair trial. And some folks allowed as to how hanging was too good for him. Still, they suspended him until dead. But the thing is, before he died he really spilled the beans on Slate. It appears that gang drifted down from up in Oklahoma with the intent of cutting out a chunk of Double Z cattle by stampeding them during this drive. It would be an inside job, so to speak. He said they got a regular wild bunch up here that was fixing to join in and complete the wrecking." He paused to catch his breath. "But now that Red nailed two of them and we know what they're up to, we can be ready for them if Slate shows his face again. The law even put a $50 bounty on his head." A couple cowhands emitted low whistles. "So Mister Boadry wanted me to warn you to be especially wary concerning your herd, and to let him know if you see anything unusual. We'll do the same for you. And the last thing he told me to do was to thank Red. If he hadn't done what he did, why then, we might all be walking into something with our eyes closed."

Red acknowledged the comment with an embarrassed nod. Surprisingly, his own thoughts had drifted to Mattie as he had come upon her during her assault. He had not forgotten and felt he probably never would forget the look on her swollen, bleeding face as he had handed her his shirt. She had been hurt, deeply. He wondered if he would ever see the return of that self-sure, confident girl he had met and given his carved horse to. Her eyes held that haunted look of one who has stared at the ugly face of death. She had been rattled to her core, for sure. But then, so had he. One thing for sure was that he did not regret for a moment killing Buck nor what happened to Turp. See Bird believed what his father had taught him, a man makes his own life and generally gets what he believes he deserves.

Talk moved on to other subjects, and Clayton was still regaling the Bar L crew with stories about their drive when See Bird decided he had heard quite enough windies for one day. It was decided Clayton would spend the night with the Bar L and head back in the morning. The rain had stopped, and the night seemed calm and quiet. The chuckles and teasing voices See Bird heard as he drifted off to sleep told him the mood and morale of the men was on the upswing again. But the last thing he saw before darkness swallowed him was a sad, bleeding face looking up in the moonlight as her hand reached out to him.

Chapter 13

"Well now Red, would you look at that and tell me if you've ever seen anything grander." Ulysses Slocum's laconic speaking style belied the intense emotion he was feeling. As they sat on the bluffs, the panorama unfolded for miles in either direction. Across the wide and braided river was Oklahoma, the land designated to be Indian country forever. The Bar L laid up on the Texas side and resupplied at Dendy's road ranch. They were now rested and in good shape for the push across the Red River and into and through that very Indian country. The Red, itself replenished by the recent rains, presented a sizable obstacle, but the two men astride their mounts had no doubt that it, too, would be overcome, as every other obstacle they had vanquished in the last month, by an application of grit, intelligence, and sheer stubbornness. See Bird could see by the trees and other debris deposited on the cut banks opposite and below them how high the water had been and was grateful that even with the recent rains, the river was not nearly as full as he had feared. He watched the water flow steadily to the east, thinking about how it would soon flow past his peoples' land, seeing in his mind where the playful Kiamichi joined its big brother.

The Double Z had taken its herd off to the west and across the Little Wichita to make its ford of the big river upstream. But after studying it in silence for a few minutes, the two riders turned and headed toward where the Bar L was bedded down, nearly two miles south. See Bird was confident from his reading of the Bar L foreman's body language that his herd would be making the crossing within sight of where they just sat.

Perhaps the cattle sensed the excitement the drovers were feeling. Perhaps, after all the wet weather lately, they were made restless by the electricity in the clearing air. Maybe they just smelled the big river. For whatever reason, the riders had a difficult time getting the herd to bed down. Just when it seemed the drovers were being successful, one animal would hear, or imagine it heard, something and stand abruptly, causing a chain reaction in those nearby. The whole group, perhaps as few as ten or as many as seventy-five would stand there and stare out into the gloom, just waiting for something to trigger them into a run. Thankfully, nothing did, and the night hawks managed to talk them all down again, singing their songs and speaking as if the anxious creatures could understand these cowboys would let nothing bad happen to them that night. Nevertheless, it was with considerable relief that Rafe saw See Bird and the second shift of riders moving alongside into place. He was just realizing how deeply tired he was and how some hot coffee and a spot to sleep without too many rocks would be all a man could want. See Bird reined up, accompanied by a still yawning Luke, and after exchanging greetings, Rafe turned around to head back to camp.

From somewhere beyond the camp fire a horse whinnied, nickered, and then began screaming in rage, its cries lancing the still night air. See Bird could only imagine what was causing the animal to behave in such a manner, and as he quickly scanned the restless cattle, he began to pray that its frenzy would soon end. All was silent for a few moments, and the two drovers were beginning to hope things would be all right. Then, piercingly, a series of enraged equine screeches filled the air, and it seemed to See Bird the entire earth suddenly rose up before him in shadowed gloom. Over three thousand one hundred panicked cattle had instantly decided that anywhere else on earth would be preferable to where they presently were and decided to get there as quickly as possible.

Since the screaming horse was to their south, the herd chose north as their path to salvation. Within seconds, the entire thirty-one-hundred plus were on the move, breaking into a run. Rafe cursed his bad luck and together with See Bird and Luke, spun his horse in pursuit of the fleeing herd.

Every Bar L man not mounted two minutes before had by now found a horse and was riding to flank the herd. Any thought of rest by the drovers coming off the first shift had dissipated like smoke amid the cries of the distressed horse and the pound of thundering hooves. Every Bar L rider available streaked alongside the herd, trying desperately to turn it, to deflect its run away from the Red River bluffs. Two miles may seem like a long way for a cow to walk, but when running, the long legged Texas cattle could cover ground like deer.

Ulysses Slocum had done this before. In spite of that, or maybe because of it, he found himself breaking out in a sweat of anxiety. He knew he was leading some fifteen riders along the left, or west flank of the herd, trying to keep pace with the panicked animals and to exert pressure along their flank in order to turn them. His sorrel was a steady horse, an intelligent and strong cow pony that responded well to what he asked of it. But even it balked at being asked to physically bump into the side of the horned steer racing alongside. With a twist of the steer's head the pony would be disemboweled and its rider thrown and most certainly killed in the hard-hooved chaos beneath. Nonetheless, maintaining a firm grip on the reins, making all the noise he could, that is exactly what the foreman did. For a few moments his tactic even appeared to be having some effect, as the racing steer veered slightly to its right, pushing up against its interior neighbor, and forcing that animal to veer as well. Slocum knew that behind him, the other riders were desperately using every trick they had ever learned or could imagine to turn this herd before it wrecked itself on the approaching bluffs.

The herd was beginning to turn. He wasn't imagining it. He was sure. The physical pressure was paying off. Then, just as quickly as a small flame of hope flickered, it was snuffed out. Slocum suddenly found himself and his horse surrounded by, and contained within the stampeding herd, as the cattle immediately following him burst through the porous wall of riders. Now, at least for the next several moments, Slocum knew he was riding, not to turn the herd but to save his own life. He had to escape those horns and hooves. As he worked his horse as quickly and carefully as he could to the outside, the mass of the herd swept him along in its thunderous passage, following its leaders toward their terrible end. He no longer believed he could prevent its destruction, but he knew he could not cease trying until it was over. His dry mouth tasted bitter in his despair. Only one more running steer barred his way to the outside flank of the herd. He spurred his tired mount to a final effort, though he knew well, even as he broke through to the outside, the chances of his regaining the front of the herd and turning the leaders were growing slimmer by the second. With a final lunge, his horse emerged from the herd and almost collided with a trio of riders flying past. He turned his horse to follow in their wake.

See Bird had not expected someone to dart out from the herd and he could not have seen Slocum even had there been more visibility than the thin quarter-moon was providing. It was pure luck they avoided a disastrous collision. But he couldn't stop to apologize now. Even as he closed on the herd leaders he could feel the slight dip in the terrain that preceded the equally slight rise to the cut-bank bluffs above the river. Whoever the brave drover was who had risked his life, he had succeeded in knocking the herd off its suicidal course slightly. But unless he could turn it the rest of the way, See Bird knew all the drovers's efforts would have been in vain.

The herd leaders sensed danger before they started up to the approaching river bluffs. But the pressure from those following made it impossible for them to stop. They slowed slightly, allowing See Bird on Kiamichi and Luke astride his favorite black to gain the corner. Rafe on his exhausted mount, bone-tired himself after spending hours riding night watch, dropped behind but was still working the herd furiously. See Bird, realizing it was now all or nothing slammed the valiant Kiamichi against the side of the leader, all the time shouting and shooting his pistol. Luke rode with his tongue glued to the roof of his mouth, trailing in See Bird's wake, firing his six-shooter into the air as they both raced the herd toward the river.

"It's turning! It's turning!" See Bird shouted into the night. "Keep it going!" But in his heart he knew his efforts would not be enough. Then the reckless ecstasy of the moment seized him as it had before, and he knew with utter certainty what he must do. Dropping the reins, he freed both hands, putting himself in perilous danger. Reloading his pistol on the fly he continued firing with his left hand. With his right he wrenched the Winchester from its scabbard. Kiamichi never faltered in his stride. One stumble, one slip, and See Bird knew it would be all over, both for himself and his horse. But he placed all his faith in his steed, and Kiamichi, drawing on hundreds of years of breeding, never missed a step, trusting implicitly in the judgment of his rider.

Luke, clinging to his reins and firing sporadically, could scarcely believe what he saw next. See Bird, a six-shooter in one hand and a Winchester in the other, was racing at breakneck speed along the edge of the bluffs, his horse kicking pebbles over its edge. Suddenly, See Bird lowered the Winchester and, with one shot, dropped the lead steer in its tracks. It cartwheeled once, rolled over, and slid to a grinding stop. Kiamichi broke to a sudden halt as if in the arena and with See Bird astride, stood at the head of the downed steer defiantly as his rider shouted and fired the Winchester into the air. Luke took what he was certain was his last look at this incredible horseman and his courageous mount just before they would be swept over the bluffs and into the swiftly running waters below. And then the miraculous happened. Poised, as it were, to trample both the downed lead steer and the fierce man sitting his horse, blocking their path, into the river, the leaders wavered and then veered to the right, leading the herd behind them, thundering within inches of the tableau etched in outline on the bluff. See Bird felt the wind churned by the herd's close passage and smelled the stink of its lathered mass, and as the adrenaline seeped from his body, was surprised to feel a sense of relief that Kiamichi would not have to die. His own fate seemed somehow unimportant.

Now all that remained was for the drovers to finish turning the entire herd in on itself, so that it would lose its forward momentum and become a milling mass of exhausted and confused cattle. See Bird maintained his position astride Kiamichi, firing his reloaded pistol and Winchester as first Luke, then Rafe, followed by the other Bar L riders rode past, flanking the herd. As quickly as the panic had started, it ended. Within minutes the herd had mostly come to a standstill, and shortly after that, with the Bar L riders walking slow circles around them, the herd started bedding down again, this time to stay for the night. The stampede, at least this one, was over, and at the cost of only one steer.

Chapter 14

"That was a close shave, Jim." Slocum addressed his typically understated remark to the man astride the horse next to him. It was morning again, and viewing the river from their vantage, the two men slouched in their saddles were deeply impressed with how near a thing the stampede had been.

Big Jim nodded. "Mighty close. If you hadn't risked your life to turn that mob I expect I'd be driving a considerably smaller herd today. And it was my own blasted fault for going this route. I should have followed the Double Z. I foolishly dropped the herd in a dangerous place. What was I thinking? I could have gotten some good men killed last night."

It was Slocum's turn to nod. He twisted one end of his mustache. "Maybe, maybe not. You couldn't have done anything about that cayuse getting tangled up in his picket rope when that rattler spooked him. But you're right about one thing. Mamas don't make men any better than these. And what can I say about Red? He dropped that bull and turned the stampede with guts and a Winchester. I've worked cattle all my life and thought I'd seen everything. But that—if I hadn't seen it with my own eyes I wouldn't have believed it." He looked directly at Big Jim. "I don't know that I believe it yet."

Big Jim chuckled, "You're right. He's not much to look at, but I'd sure want to have him on my side in a pinch. The man's right handy."

"That's a fact." One of the sinkers he had eaten for breakfast must have gotten caught in his throat because he felt the urge to clear it. Then, directing his gaze down toward the river where a crew of cowboys was flailing away at some timbers along its bank, he asked, "Now what in tarnation is taking those boys so long to build a measly raft? How can men look so smooth handling horses and so awkward swinging axes? I guess I'll just ride on down and make sure they're using the right end." With that, the foreman kicked his horse to a trot. Big Jim watched him ride away and felt a sudden wave of gratitude wash through his being. That men such as these would sacrifice so much for so little, and give their loyalty so unstintingly made him proud beyond telling. Before his own throat choked up he spun his horse and headed away. Cookie had better get in gear, he thought. If we are to get the entire herd and wagons across the Red and put some serious miles between it and tonight's camp, well then things had better get a move on pretty quick.

"Boys, you oughta stop beating that wood to death and use the blade a bit more." Slocum tilted his hat back on his head and smiled.

"Now caporal, you really oughtn't say such a hurtful thing." Sanchez rejoined in an injured tone. "We've nearly finished with this beautiful ship, so soon to be launched, right amigos?" This was greeted by a chorus of affirmative profanities. "We will name her the Carmen, after my dear aunt—who drowned in the Rio Grande when she drank a little bit too much tequila. I just hope this Carmen floats better than she did." A chorus of derisive hoots and laughs greeted this comment.

"Dalton, help Luke set that last log in place." Rafe was speaking and it was clear he wanted to finish this job as soon as possible so he could get his men back to real cowboying. "We'll lash it to the others under the hoodlum wagon there. That should give it enough buoyancy. You can see Red on the other side of the river, Mister Slocum," he continued. "He and a few others already swam the river twice and have the other end of the rope tied up to their horses. When you give the word they'll tow the whole contraption across. This end is secured so the raft and wagon don't head off down stream. Pretty slick, huh?" As he spoke Dalton and Luke worked the last log into place and tied it to the others. The slack was taken out of the rope. "On your command, sir." Rafe executed a passable salute. Slocum eyed the finished product. Crude, he thought, but it should work. So far they had been able to walk across the rivers they encountered; this was the first river that required a boat. And after the Red, there should not be any others. He stood in his stirrups and waved his hat at the rider on the other bank, who immediately began walking his horse away from the river. The rope grew taut, the wagon resisted for a moment as its wheels came completely free of the river bed. Then, as smoothly as if it had a silent motor, the raft drifted just a bit down stream and then headed directly for the opposite bank.

"Looks good, men. And just in time." Slocum turned in his saddle. "I might be mistaken but I think I hear the chuck wagon coming."

And so the crossing of the Red River began. After the wagons and all the goods that could be ferried across were unloaded on the Oklahoma side, the remuda was brought up. The saddle horses would be used as leaders for the crossing. The cattle, hopefully, would follow. No one considered reluctant drovers. But when Little Billy caught a look at the Red and was told he would have to swim it with his horse, he blanched as white as a sheet. "I'm sorry. I just didn't know it was this big. I can't swim a stroke. I just know for certain I'll drown. I just can't do it." And he started to back away in terror. Nothing anybody could say would reassure the distraught boy. Finally, Slocum ordered the raft brought back one more time. And with Billy clinging desperately on all fours and with a few more items the men wanted to keep dry aboard, the raft made its final passage.

After all the time spent constructing the raft and ferrying the wagons, the crossing by the herd was almost anticlimactic. The saddle horses, trailed by the cattle, were funneled down a ravine to the river several hundred yards upstream, where the river was split into several channels, only one of which required swimming. The horses plunged right in, and with their nearly naked riders swimming alongside, made short work of the crossing. Following the horses and pressured by the herd, the leading cattle splashed in quickly and only a few minutes later were exiting from the river downstream, not far above where the wagons had made their earlier crossing. The swimming herd, pressured by the river's current, had formed into a crescent with its tips anchored on either bank and the body bowed slightly below the exit. Scarcely a half-hour passed before all the horses, cowboys and cattle were safely on the Oklahoma side and moving steadily up and away from the mighty Red and into the interior of Indian country.

There was no doubt in any of the drovers' minds when they pitched camp that evening that even though they were only about six miles from the river, they definitely were in another country. The long grasses whispering in the prairie wind bespoke a land where, until recently, the only thunder of hooves to be heard had been caused by the migration of countless buffalo, the last of which had been slaughtered to feed the railroad workers and as a conscious decision on the part of the American government to bring the independent plains people to their knees.

Traces of the buffalo, so newly removed from the scene, remained in the very trail See Bird and the Bar L crew were following. Named after Jesse Chisholm, the trail he pioneered had actually been long known and used, both by the migrating buffalo and by the indigenous people seeking the easiest route from north to south across what was to become Oklahoma. From the Red River in the south to Caldwell, Kansas, the trail followed good terrain, and the few rivers that must be crossed were all easily fordable.

As See Bird rode the perimeter of the peacefully bedded herd, the distant howl of a wolf carried with it a sense of peace to his soul that he had seldom felt in his years of cowboying. The Milky Way, another trail, draped itself across the night sky. He reined in his horse and sat silently for a few moments, letting the prairie night work its magic on him. Back when See Bird was a child, his Sunday school teacher, Miss Tarkenton, taught him all about the Garden of Eden. Even Adam walking with God, he thought, could not have been closer to his creator than See Bird felt this night. I may not even own the horse I ride, he thought. But then why do I feel like the richest man in the world? Unable to answer his own question, he nudged his horse forward and resumed his watch. Somewhere across the herd a clear cowboy tenor was singing something sad about a town called Laredo.

Chapter 15

"Red, look at that, will you?" It was Slocum pointing off to his left. See Bird turned and watched a pair of antelope graze in a swale not more than a hundred yards off, completely unafraid of their human neighbors. "Do you think you could put that Winchester to good use? Some fresh meat would be a nice change of pace from what we've been eating lately."

"I think I might oblige," See Bird said as he raised the rifle from its scabbard. Slowly he drew down on the unsuspecting pair and squeezed the trigger. Both antelope leaped at the sound, but while one disappeared over a low ridge, the other fell as if poleaxed. "From the way those two reacted, I'd be surprised if the other one's gone very far. It's probably just on the other side of that ridge there. I'll check it out—shouldn't take long."

Slocum nodded and remained where he was, glancing over his right shoulder at the herd moving slowly along, prodded by the flankers. Several cows thought the grass looked greener where they weren't and tried to break off from the herd. A cowboy, Slocum couldn't see just who, danced his pony off and headed the wayward cattle. Slocum glanced back over at See Bird, who had reached the downed antelope, glanced at it, and was now disappearing behind the low ridge into the neighboring valley. Clearly, the herd required his attention more than Red, he thought, so he turned his horse back in that direction.

See Bird had been right. The second antelope had dashed over the ridge only to resume grazing as if nothing were amiss, scarcely two hundred yards from where he shot its companion. However, instead of drawing a bead on the animal, See Bird slid the rifle back in its sheath and stared at what appeared in the small valley just beyond it. A small herd of perhaps forty or fifty of what surely looked like Texas cattle were slowly grazing their way south. He considered for a moment if perhaps they were just some range cattle wandering by but dismissed the thought. He had seen no evidence of local herds for two days, and besides, they were bunched up tighter than range cattle would have been.

Kicking his horse into a gentle canter, he descended into the swale, finally startling the second antelope into flight. But he scarcely noticed. His attention was fixed on the mystery cattle. It was but a minute's work to identify the brand. Just as he had feared, they were Double Z stock. Clearly Randle's outfit had met some misfortune. It was short work to turn the small herd and push them toward the Bar L drive. He paused only long enough to hoist the downed antelope across Kiamichi's back.

Watching See Bird approach, driving the small herd, Slocum twisted the end of his handlebar moustache in curiosity. Unable to wait for his arrival, the trail boss spurred his mount out to meet him. "Lord, Red. I knew you were hungry, but this is plumb ridiculous. What do you have there?" he asked as he joined in to push the cattle forward.

"Looks like some trouble hit the Double Z. This bunch was wandering south, trying to get back to Texas, I suppose. Their herd must have stampeded yesterday or the night before. I expect we'll see a rider soon."

"Probably," the foreman responded, "but if they're this scattered, I'm afraid they'll have their hands full just trying to round them up again. We'll bring the Bar L up here and stop for the day. It don't make sense to push on and get all tangled up with Boadry's bunch or whatever's left of them. Why don't you and Luke ride on ahead and see what's up, see if they need any help? I'll have the boys look around for any other Double Z strays they can round up. Just drop that little deer over at the chuck wagon. Too bad you boys won't get any venison." They both laughed.

Luke was glad for the break in the tedium. The day seemed made for riding through the open country alongside his friend on an errand of mercy. "You came from up in these parts didn't you, Red," he asked as they walked briskly along.

"Over to the east," See Bird waved a hand. "This land belongs to the Kiowa, Comanche, Apache—those folks. My peoples' country is hillier with forests and many more streams than this. And more cattle, too. The Choctaw are one of the "civilized" tribes. Anything the white man can do, we learn to do and then do it better." His comment was intended to be humorous, but Luke wondered to himself if, knowing See Bird as he did, it wasn't more than just a little bit true. He smiled to himself but said nothing.

A bit later See Bird said, "Let's take a little detour to the west. That bunch of cattle I found came from that direction. There may be more of them. If so, we can just scoop them up and take them back to their rightful owners."

Luke agreed and the two riders swung off to the west, angling north, crossing several small ridges. As they crested one, what they saw took their breath away. Down in the valley, grunting and swishing their tails, grazed a small herd of nearly twenty buffalo. The two men backed their horses below the crest, concealing them from view, dismounted, and without saying a word, slouched back up and dropped prone, peering over the ridge line through the long grass at this scene from a bygone era. The thought of killing the magnificent beasts, if considered at all, was immediately dismissed as impractical, given their distance from the Bar L herd and the impossibility of slaughtering, cleaning, and transporting such a beast.

Just when they were about to rise and resume their quest for strays, from around the base of a small knob opposite their position and to the south rode a lone horseman. Upon spotting the small herd of buffalo, he raised his rifle to the sky and cried out in triumph. His brown and white spotted pony seemed hardly large enough to carry its burden. Nevertheless, it burst into a gallop and then a run, directly at the startled herd.

"I don't believe it. Do you believe what we're seeing, Red?"

"Hush up now, Luke, and watch." The buffalo hunter, clad in fringed buckskins with a dirty white bandana tied around his head, carried an old rifle in one hand. A powderhorn was draped around his neck and under one arm. Slim as a reed, he rode as though a very part of his mount, controlling it, as he did, with his knees and mocassined heels.

"What's he doing, Red? Is he trying to shoot himself in the head?"

"I've never seen this, Luke," See Bird whispered, transfixed, "but my people have talked of it. Do you see that old rifle he's using? He carries the bullet in his mouth and spits it into the barrel. Watch now." The rider, racing alongside a big bull, removed the barrel from his mouth and slammed the stock of the rifle down on the saddle. "That lodges the bullet in the barrel so he doesn't have to stop and use a ramrod." With both hands entirely free, the hunter seemed to float above the back of his horse. Slowly he lowered the rifle, aimed at the bull racing alongside, and fired a single shot. The hairy creature went to his knees as if in prayer and slid forward a ways before coming to a stop. The rest of the small herd rumbled off to the north. "Let's make ourselves scarce. If a hunter is here, that means there will be many other people nearby. We may not be welcome guests." The two young men backed cautiously down from the crest and remounted their horses, walking them down the slope and away from the scene of the hunt. Both scanned the countryside carefully for sign of anyone else but saw nothing. They rode in silence back to the east a ways before swinging northward again, lost in their own thoughts, Luke shivering in excitement at the wild savagery he had just been witness to, and See Bird, proud to the core at his sense of kinship with the skilled hunter and yet somehow saddened by the abyss of experience that lay between them.

After an hour of steady riding north the two drovers had picked up a few strays wearing the Double Z brand when See Bird spotted an approaching rider. The pistol on his hip was loaded but his glance naturally fell on the Winchester first. A moment later Luke saw the rider as well and the two of them stopped driving the strays and warily let their mounts slide apart a few yards. The oncoming rider noticed their movement and slowed his approach to a walk.

"Howdy, friend," See Bird said.

"Howdy back atcha," the dusty rider responded. "Looks like you got yourselves a few cows there. We just lost a few."

"And who might you be?" See Bird asked.

"Me, they call Quicksilver. My outfit's the Double Z—just back a piece." He gestured with one hand. "You look familiar. Ain't you that hot shot rider for the Bar L, Red somethingorother? We met tossing ropes at a fence."

Red relaxed a bit and smiled. "Yeah, that's me. And this is Lucky Luke. He rides for the brand, too." Quicksilver nodded in Luke's direction. Luke smiled at Red's familiarity. "We bumped into about three or four dozen head wearing the Double Z and figured you'd had some trouble. We were just on our way to see if we could be of assistance—picked up a few more on the way."

"I'm obliged to you for that, Red. We sure enough got hit the night before last. Cattle stampeded all over hell's half acre. As of this morning we're still nearly a couple hundred short. Great country for losing cattle. Boys, I've enjoyed this little chat, but I gotta get back to work. Why don't you two push these and whatever else you can find on up the trail? I'll go on down to your outfit and fill 'em in with what I know."

"Sounds good to me." See Bird touched the brim of his hat. "We'll see you later." Quicksilver did the same and, touching spurs to his mount, passed the two and continued on down the trail toward the Bar L herd.

Just as dusk was approaching, the two riders, trailing eight cows, caught up with the Double Z. They were met by the foreman, Boadry, who led the two tired cowboys in to the camp. As they sat holding plates of steak and beans they recounted what they knew and were filled in by the Double Z foreman on the stampede.

"At first we thought it might have been wolves. Everything was quiet, except for their howling. We're so danged shorthanded that Morgan drew the short straw and was riding night hawk. He said he thought he saw a wolf pack shadowing the herd." Boadry stopped talking.

"You said 'at first,'" Luke interjected. "What did you mean by that?"

The narrow-faced man looked at Luke with a face, Luke thought that showed cunning if not a great intelligence. "Some things feel right, and some don't. Why didn't anyone else see wolves? And why haven't we found any traces of them or their bloody work since? I just don't know."

See Bird leaned in, setting his empty plate on the ground. "Oh, there were wolves, all right. Only they were the two legged kind." Boadry stared at him, uncomprehending. See Bird continued. "Before he was sent to his maker, Turpin told the law there was another man working for Slate in your crew and the whole idea had been to rustle the Double Z on this drive. Isn't that a fact? Sure, Turp and Buck are dead, but Slate high tailed it, and now you got wolves. Who's this Morgan, and what do you know about him?"

Boadry ran a callused hand through his thick black hair, as he finally started piecing together the puzzle. "I don't think… but still I hired him about the same time I hired Slate. We needed help for the roundup. Seemed to be a steady worker, never caused any problems. But…" The troubled foreman pondered for a moment longer and then made up his mind. "Clayton, go fetch Morg and bring him here, whether he wants to or not. And you might want to take someone else with you."

Clayton rose and left. Boadry turned to See Bird. "Seems like I really messed up. When I get back to Texas, if Mister Randle will keep me on, and what you say pans out…" He nodded. "I'll owe you one, Red."

The men drank coffee in silence until the sound of horses' hooves let them know they had company. A nervous-looking nondescript cowboy dismounted and walked over to the campfire. He glanced briefly at the two strangers seated on the ground near the fire before he turned his attention to his foreman. "What's this all about, boss? Clayton drags me out of my bedroll and I'm about done in from riding night hawk last night and then chasing strays all day."

Boadry spoke without looking up. "You're done here, Morgan. I been putting one and one together and they point at you. I don't need to explain myself to you, but I'll say this much. I hired you and trusted you. In return you stabbed the Double Z in the back." Morgan started to protest but Boadry talked him down, staring up at him now. "Your buddy Turpin spilled his guts before they strung him up." Morgan flinched. See Bird glanced Boadry's way and saw a cunning light in his eyes. It was the look of a man who knows what he said just struck pay dirt. Morgan's eyes now flicked from one man to another around the fire. He seemed to want to look anywhere except directly at his foreman's eyes. "That's a dirty lie. He had no proof."

"Maybe not," Boadry continued and slowly stood, dusting his pants. "But this ain't no court of law. Here I am the judge and jury. I'm giving you fair notice, Morgan. You've got ten minutes to collect your gear and get out of here or I personally will kill you for the stinking rustler you are."

"You can't talk to me that way. I…"

The foreman pulled his revolver and pointed it at Morgan's stunned face. "You're wasting time. I'm counting. You see, I may not be as smart as some people, but once I figure out the score, I'm the dog that bites and won't let go." He smiled grimly.

"But my pay," he objected. "You owe me…" Morgan abruptly shut up when he heard the hammer cock on the big pistol in Boadry's hand. He saw Luke and See Bird rise and stand beside the foreman while he knew Clayton stood somewhere to his rear. Sweat ran in rivulets down his grimy face.

"Collect your pay from Slate. But you'd better do it quick. If I find him I'm going to kill him. Tell him that. Now you only have eight minutes left."

Suddenly Morgan spun on his heels and walked away, fists clenched. A few minutes later the men heard the galloping hoof beats of a lone horse fade into the night.

See Bird understood now why Josh Randle had hired Boadry to run his outfit. The man didn't look like much, that was for sure, but he had grit and persistence. Earlier that evening he had told the Double Z riders they would remain where they were until all the cattle were accounted for, and no one had doubted his intent. On the other hand, as it seemed likely that, short of stumbling onto Slate's crew and the rustled cattle, they would have to stay here forever, Boadry was now rethinking his options.

Rubbing the stubble on his chin, Clayton spoke. "That was mighty cool of you to call out Morgan like that. I didn't know Turp had fingered him."

"He didn't. I just took a shot in the dark. Looks like it found its target." Boadry's small black eyes stared across the fire. "But we're still short nearly one hundred and seventy-five head. At ten dollars per, that's a pile of money."

"I expect when you add in what you find tomorrow and what the Bar L brings up, that'll be cut down quite a bit." See Bird paused and then added, "By now Slate's got that bunch as far from here as possible and will sell them as fast as he can."

Boadry punched his knee, "Tomorrow we'll cut for his trail. I'll follow him 'til hell freezes over."

Clayton protested, "But what are we gonna do with the herd in the meantime?"

See Bird pursed his lips and spoke with a decisiveness he was not quite sure he felt himself. "Forget cutting for his trail. You'll only be too late. I figure he's going to want to unload that stock quick as possible. There's nothing back the way we came or to the east anywhere close. So he has to go north or west, toward Kansas or to Fort Sands. You send a couple riders north to Caldwell as fast as they can ride. Luke and me will head to Fort Sands. I'm not a betting man, but I'd lay odds he's going to one of those two places. We get there first and tell the authorities what's going on. If we get the army's help we can bag the whole lot of them and get the cattle back to boot. Send a rider back to tell Big Jim what's going on. You can sit here for another day to collect strays if need be. I don't reckon anyone's behind us on the trail this late in the year."

As See Bird spoke, he noticed a change in the demeanor of the Double Z trail boss. His sense of despair and ruin had given way to hope. When See Bird finished, Boadry spoke, "Red, you make good sense. That just might work, if you'd do that for us."

"We'll do it, all right. But it ain't just for you. Good folks have been hurt plenty by this snake. And if he squirms loose here, he'll hurt more, maybe worse. So we've got a stake in it. And if my partner's willing, we'll be riding west by dawn."

"You can sure count me in," Luke said. "I wouldn't miss this for the world."

Boadry wrapped things up. "Clayton, you and Lem head for Caldwell first thing in the morning. Slate's got two days on us already. But you won't be pushing steers, so you should get there first if you don't delay. You boys get a good night's sleep. I'll have the old woman rustle up some grub early. I'll ride a night shift tonight, so you can be fresh. We'll wait to pick up whatever beeves the Bar L found, and then we'll move out. I figure to be meeting up with you in about a week somewhere up the trail. Red, we'll look for any word from you once we get to Caldwell." With that the meeting broke up, Clayton to find and inform Lem of the plan, Boadry to his horse, and See Bird and Luke to their bedrolls.

Chapter 16

By dawn, the riders had already put several miles between themselves and the last night's camp. Luke and See Bird rode with the newly risen sun warming their backs as their horses walked quickly through the long grass. Luke took a swallow from his canteen and wiped his mouth with the back of his hand. "Now I know what we're doing is the right thing and all, but still, I've learned a few things lately and what I want to know, Mister Carpenter, is why you're going so almighty far out of your way to help chase down a bunch of lost cows that belong to a white man who never did your people no favors a-tall."

See Bird breathed deeply and said, "Luke, listen to what you just said—'my people,' and the 'white man.'" He paused to put his thoughts in order. "I look at me and just see a man. I look at you and see the same. But when you look at me you see an Indian. When you look at yourself you see a 'good' white man. Well then, I'll put this in terms you'll understand. Your law is all there is that protects me and my 'people' from being rubbed out by the likes of scum buckets like Slate. If his ilk wins out, I lose. But so do you. If 'good' people of any color don't stand up to Slate's likes, you'll suffer too. So, red or white don't matter much. It's right and wrong that counts. So I will do what I can to defend your white man's law." Irritated at having to explain something he felt should have been obvious he continued, "Now, we've been jawing enough to hold us the rest of the morning. Slate's probably pushed those cows to Colorado by now. Let's pick up the pace a bit." He nudged the ribs of his mount with spurless boots. "Kiamichi, you could use some exercise. Let's run it out a bit." He reached forward and patted the side of Kiamichi's neck, and the eager horse responded with a mile-eating gallop. Luke on his black kept pace.

By noon they had crossed another branch of the Chisholm Trail. The cowboys knew that what was called the Chisholm Trail was actually a network of parallel and interconnected trails. As Luke gathered some wood for a fire, See Bird stopped him. "I don't expect anyone has spotted us yet, but if Slate is smart at all he'll have somebody watching his back trail. We may be miles off, north or south, but let's not take any chances. I don't have a hankering to tangle with his crew. Wherever they are, I just want to beat them to Fort Sands and let the army take care of them. So if you don't mind, let's just run a cold camp for a couple more days. I figure by then, wherever they are, we oughta be ahead of them."

A bit disappointed, Luke dropped the wood he was carrying and squatted beside See Bird. "I guess I can do without the brown gargle, but I kind of miss a fire. It makes a soul feel sorta homey, if you get my drift."

See Bird nodded in agreement but said nothing. From his saddle bags, he withdrew a can of peaches the cook had stowed for them along with other goodies to eat along the trail. Using the point and blade of his big knife adeptly, See Bird opened the can, took a big swallow and passed it to his companion. "Looks like we'll not suffer too much, though." Luke smiled.

As evening of the third day descended, See Bird looked for a spot to rest for the night. All about him, before and behind, stretched the wide grasslands of western Oklahoma. The grass was noticeably shorter, and the air smelled drier somehow, and spicier. As he sat on Kiamichi, surveying the scene, the mount nickered and tossed its head. "What's that, boy? Do you hear something, a wolf maybe?" The sorrel quieted but stood staring into the dusk, his ears pointed to the northwest. See Bird started the horse forward, up a slight rise when his attention was riveted by the sound of a sharp crack, as if a large branch had suddenly snapped. He stopped, listened but for a moment and then swung the horse around and quickly made his way back to where Luke had dismounted and started to remove his saddle gear from the back of his horse.

See Bird jumped from his horse and pulled Luke down into a squat. "Leave it, Luke," See Bird hissed between clenched teeth. "We aren't stopping here. Company's just over that little knob. And out here I got a pretty good idea who it is. Let's just sneak up there and take a peek, see if we recognize anybody. Then we'll give them a wide berth and be on our way." See Bird silently slipped the Winchester from off Kiamichi, and with Luke at his heels, swiftly ascended the rise. The purple residue of the sunset was already giving way to the first stars as the men topped the ridge. There, below them, flowed a little stream, where three men had pitched a small camp. In the dim light, See Bird guessed there to be about two dozen horses picketed nearby, on the other side of the small stream. The fire was considerably larger than was needed for so small a camp, but that was not what See Bird's attention was focused on. The sound of another sharp crack, accompanied by a stream of curses, met his and Luke's ears. Two of the men were holding the ends of ropes tied to the legs and neck of a horse they were struggling to keep on the ground. A third man was walking around the horse, with a whip in his hand, continually cursing and periodically snapping the big whip down on the back or any other vulnerable area of the tormented horse he could reach. See Bird took in the scene for a few moments and then, tugging at Luke's shirt sleeve, backed over and down the hill they had climbed only a few minutes before.

When they reached their horses, See Bird asked, "Did you recognize any of those hombres?"

"No sir," Luke's voice quivered, "but watching that man beat that helpless horse makes my blood boil. What do you make of it all?"

See Bird stood by his horse, loosely holding the reins in his hands. "The way I see it is this. Those men are part of Slate's gang. They sure don't need all those horses for just three men. My guess is that not too far from here is the outlaw's main camp, and if we nosed around, we'd bump into a lot of beeves that shouldn't be here. Don't ask me how come we stumbled onto them. If that hombre hadn't been so intent on torturing that horse, we might have accidentally ridden right in. And I'm not so sure we would have ridden out again. Now we can get on our horses and scoot around to the left. By dawn we could be well away from here and them none the wiser."

Luke kicked some dirt but said nothing. "Or," See Bird continued, "We could have us a little fun before we ride out."

Luke raised his eyes to meet those of his partner. "What do you have in mind?"

Seeing Luke's willingness to take the more dangerous path brought a tight lipped smile to See Bird's face. "I have never been able to stomach a man that treats a poor dumb animal so mean. It gives human beings a bad name. We don't know these men, and they don't know us. The last thing they'd expect would be for us to ride right in. We could make things a little hot for Slate and his crew. What do you say?"

"Red, if you hadn't said what you just did, I'd have figured I didn't know you so well as I thought I did. Those men make me so mad I'd do anything."

"You don't have to do anything. Just follow my lead. Mount up, and stay about ten to fifteen yards to my right and back just a bit so's they have trouble seeing you. Say nothing, and we just might bust up their little party and give Slate something to gnaw on until the army finishes him off. Let's go."

Without another word, the two men stepped into the stirrups again and turned their stout-hearted horses up the small hill. Luke peeled off and rode over to the right, as instructed. As they crested the rise and started down the hill toward the fire, the three men below were so intent on their devilish work that they failed to see that company had dropped in until See Bird drew to a halt and spoke, still beyond the light of the fire.

"Mister," he called from the dark. He waited until the man wielding the whip turned his face in his direction. "You like to have ruined a good horse. Why don't you just set that whip down and you two other men just get up and drop your gun belts."

"You must be crazy, stranger, riding in here all alone and giving us orders." He stared into the gathering gloom, barely able to make out the image of a man sitting his horse. He turned to the two startled men still at the ropes. "Boys, stay where you are. I'm gonna teach this horse a lesson, and then we'll deal with this busybody. He raised his whip hand and brought the length of it down across the quivering flesh of the tormented mustang.

A note of anger hardened See Bird's voice. "Mister, you try that one more time, and it'll be the last time you ever whip a horse." His words were punctuated by the snap of his Winchester levering a round into the chamber. "And who says I'm alone? Bill, Sam, pull off left and right." Taking his cue, Luke made his movement to the right noisily.

Now, obviously worried by the turn in the situation, but unwilling to concede, the man with the whip glanced at his two compatriots who clearly were having second thoughts about their exposed situation. "You two stay right where you are," he ordered nervously, "or you'll answer to me!" He then turned his attention back to See Bird and tried a laugh that sounded more like a cough. "As for you, after I'm done with this cayuse, come on in and we'll have us a little parley. What are you gonna do, shoot a man for whipping his own horse?" He raised the whip and turned back to the helpless animal.

The crack of the Winchester split the night air, and at the same moment the whip went flying from the man's hand. "Oh, God! Oh Jesus! He shot my hand. I got no thumb. The man who a moment before had blustered so confidently now collapsed to the ground, reduced to a blubbering whimperer.

"Bill, Sam, hold your fire!" See Bird ordered into the darkness. "Now you other boys untie that horse and let it go." Seeing what had happened to their leader and suspecting other unseen assailants, the two rushed to comply. The desperate mustang stumbled to her feet, gained stability, and took off into the darkness. "Keep your hands where we can see them. You had your fun. Now we'll have ours." The two men shifted their feet, fearful of the authoritative voice from the dark. "Real carefully, drop your gun belts and get that one from your boss there, too. I don't think he'll be needing his any time soon." Very slowly, the two obeyed again. "Now I want you to remove your boots and drop your pants. And help your boss out of his."

"Now just a gol-darned minute," one started to protest.

The crisp snap of the lever action on the Winchester silenced his protestations, and in the silence could be heard the sound of Luke cocking his pistol as well. "Buddy, maybe you didn't hear the man," the young cowboy hissed from the shadows. "You've seen him shoot. I'd do what he says, if I were you."

Seething with resentment and anger, but helpless to resist, the two shucked their boots and pants as instructed. In a few seconds they stood barefoot in their skivvies, while the man who formerly held the whip hand still sat cradling his wounded hand, rocking on the ground.

"Next, I want you to gather up all your guns, boots, and pants, and toss them into that fire. Do it now!" Once again the two leaped to obey the commanding voice from beyond the fire light. The denim caught fire quickly, and a few seconds later the bullets started cooking off, forcing the three nearly naked men to hobble off seeking cover. "Let's go, boys!" See Bird shouted into the darkness and, as bullets sprayed like popcorn from the fire, he led Luke on a gallop into the blackness and toward the picketed horses. It took only seconds to free the anxious steeds and, with shouts and shots, to drive them off into the night.

Several hundred yards away See Bird reined to a halt. Luke was quickly beside him. "Whooey! If that don't beat all! We sure enough ho-rawed that crew." Luke's delight was uncontainable. "When them bullets started cooking, those old boys took off riding a shank's mare. And that was the slickest thing I ever saw, you shooting that whip right out of that gump's hand—and by firelight, to boot! Whooey!"

"I gotta admit, that sure was a lot more fun than sneaking around them. Now they're on foot, unshucked, no boots or guns, and one with a messed up whip hand. Plus, they've got no idea who we are or how many men faced them. I think we can ride a bit easier now. I doubt they'll be coming after us tonight. Most likely, they'll think they were set on by another bunch as crooked as themselves. By dawn, in this country, they'll never track us, even if they wanted to—which I doubt they do. It'll take them half a day just to find their horses. Now that's what I call a good night's work." Checking the friendly stars, See Bird unerringly headed west, and the two men rode on, ever nearer to their destination.

Chapter 17

Except for the old warrior Geronimo, holding out in the mountains of Mexico with a handful of die hards, the days of the wars with the Comanche and Apache peoples were swiftly passing. A small community of settlers, traders, and Indians had sprung up around the outpost known as Fort Sands. Whereas in years past the role of the army had been to control and restrict the Indians to assigned reservations, nowadays it spent more time trying to stem, or at least control what had been a trickle, but was now becoming a flood of land-hungry whites, as they poured into land that by treaty was supposed to belong to the Indians.

Captain James Anderson, the commander of Company A, of the Seventh Cavalry, was an intelligent man who graduated from West Point, but with no wars to fight, resigned himself to the fact that any advancement in the army was bound to be glacially slow. An ambitious man, he chafed at that knowledge. At one time he followed the news of Sitting Bull, the old Ogallala chief, as he returned from Canada to a reservation in the Dakotas. But there seemed to be little chance of action from that direction either. It was even rumored that Bill Cody, the Wild West Show huckster, was negotiating with Sitting Bull to go on tour with his troupe. As Captain Anderson carefully drew the blade of the razor down his cheek, he wondered if it was to be his lot to disappear without a trace in this godforsaken outpost, where the only breaks from the mind-numbing boredom usually came from settling some conflict between aggrieved post Indians and the increasingly assertive settlers. The white squatters were now so numerous as to outnumber the natives who used to control this land. A number of them had even tried to organize a real town and hire their own city law enforcement. They felt the army was too cozy with the Indians. The irony was not lost on the young captain of the rebuilt Seventh Cavalry.

It was with a hint of irritation, therefore, that he saluted his aide, Lieutenant Cartwright, who swung in beside him as he emerged from his quarters and turned on the boardwalk to head for his office. As they walked, the aide explained that two dusty cowboys just rode in with a tale of rustlers on the Chisholm Trail, and these same rustlers were bringing their stolen merchandise to sell at the fort.

The two cowhands who were waiting in his sparsely furnished headquarters office rose to greet him and then waited until he was seated at his desk. It was obvious one of the cowboys was an Indian, but that did not concern the captain. Nowadays, that was a fairly common occurrence as the more intelligent of the aborigines increasingly adapted to civilization. Perhaps someday, he mused, they would completely blend in and there would be no Indians at all. Somehow that thought saddened him. He dismissed the idea as irrelevant and leaned forward on his elbows as the two cowboys on the other side of his desk told their story and then answered his questions. Yes, indeed, he thought as the interview was concluded, perhaps the day would not be as boring as he had feared.

Slate was troubled. And when he was troubled about something he usually followed his hunches. Up until now, they had served him well, at least well enough to keep him alive in a dangerous country. He had listened to the tale his three wranglers had spun, and frankly he did not know what to believe. They swore they had been suddenly attacked in the night by a large group of unknown assailants. They had fought back as best they could and thought they might have hit one of them, before Rooster had been shot in the hand. However, Slate did not join in the laughter and taunting the rest of his gang heaped on the unfortunate trio as they told how they were then humiliated by being forced to strip and run away.

The general consensus was the attack had been executed by Joshua Taggart's gang, rumored to be operating in the area. Surely, there was no way the drovers from the outfit they recently raided would have left their herd untended and come all this way only to embarrass a few of his men. And if they were from that cow outfit, why didn't they try to reclaim their cattle? They hit in the dark of night. It was obviously a well planned foray. They could probably have successfully pulled it off. No, he decided, it most likely was just a raid by another gang of rustlers and outlaws. Still, it was confusing and it troubled him. And when he felt troubled, his survival instinct took over.

"Ok, boys, listen up. I said listen up!" he roared and drew his revolver. The raucous laughter and teasing died down. Slate spun the cylinder on the revolver as he talked.

That way he knew he had his men's attention. He once shot a man point blank who dared to directly challenge a decision he made. He had been angry at Old Snake, for sure, but mainly he shot him to show the rest of the men he would brook no insolence. "You heard the story from our little ladies here. And most likely it's as they say. Most likely it was just a raid by Taggart to tell us to get out of what he calls his territory. If it was, we got to make sure he don't try that again. This here's big enough land for two gangs, plenty of cattle and not much to be seen of John Law. So here's what we're gonna do. At daybreak I'm going to head south, find Taggart, and work out a deal. Blackie will be in charge while I'm gone. We've collected enough 'strays' out here to drive on into Fort Sands, sell and make a handsome profit. I hear the good folks there are willing to pay a pretty penny for prime beef. We're only two days out so we'll all meet at the hideout in one week to divvy up shares. You got that, Blackie? If anybody gets greedy, you kill him."

The one called Blackie smiled, but the smile provided little pleasure to those who viewed it. His mouth, when he opened it, was a cavern of rotten and tobacco-stained teeth. Even among men as hardened as these, there was something corrupt and evil about his appearance. It was from this feature he had earned his name. He knew it and in a twisted way, was proud of it. "That would be no problem, boss. I don't think we'll have any problem at all."

Slate nodded. Blackie would never be a good leader, but for some reason, he had given his most precious possession, his loyalty, to the outlaw chief. Though utterly ruthless himself, he would die before he would break his code. Also, he was fast. He had hooked up with Slate following a shooting where he had outdrawn and shot two men before they could clear leather. The rest of Slate's gang knew this fact well, and though they loathed Blackie, they respected his skills and feared him.

"Mister Carpenter," Captain Anderson addressed See Bird as his equal in command as they prepared for the confrontation to come. Luke, along with Lieutenant Reilly and the two company squad leaders were present for this planning session. Luke had grown accustomed to seeing the black men in the blue uniforms as they went about the fort on their errands or rode in from patrols. He heard the Buffalo Soldiers were common enough in the West and had also heard of the courage they displayed in the late Indian wars. Still, the presence of these two very black men in such a planning session made him uncomfortable. If anyone else felt the same way, they failed to show it. "Our scout reports the herd in question is heading directly for the fort, just as you described. They would appear to muster thirteen men to bring in some two hundred head. Either they are very poor cowhands, to require so many men, or they are in fact a bandit group, as you claim." He turned to the two black men. "Sergeant Cribbs will lead the first platoon, Sergeant Jeffers the second." The two NCOs nodded. "That will leave only the third platoon, with twenty-three men to man the fort and maintain order. But I am confident that two platoons will be more than enough to do the job. Now, here is how I want the men deployed." The five men pored over a hastily drawn map that lay on the commander's desk and listened intently as he outlined the plan he and Red had developed.

Shortly after dawn the next day those early risers, from among the settlers and Indians who still clustered around the fort, were treated to a sight they had not seen much of lately. Two files of grim-faced blue-clad Buffalo Soldiers, led by the captain accompanied by two civilians, issued from the mouth of Fort Sands and passed with a jingling of spurs and the thudding of hooves between the makeshift buildings and out toward the rising sun.

It was still only mid morning when they reached their destination, a shallow rock-strewn ravine that pulled up from a small stream which obviously had been forded many times. The signs of traffic identified this crossing as the main trail running east-west from the fort. Here the soldiers deployed and settled in to await the arrival of Slate's gang.

It was only a few hours later that a cloud of dust announced the approach of the stolen herd. The orders were clear. No one was to fire until and unless they were fired upon or the order to fire was given. They were to arrest these men if at all possible. But if they resisted arrest they were to be cut down like dogs.

As Blackie and the unwary gang pushed the herd forward to cross the creek they were surprised but not alarmed to see two men there, blocking their way, sitting on their horses and looking as if they had not a care in the world. One was a small dark man in a tall black hat, astride a sturdy sorrel. The other was a rangy looking fair-skinned man, wearing a smile and riding a big black. He spoke first as Blackie was about to start the herd across. "Hold it right there, gents. We need to have us a little parley."

Blackie noticed that both men's hands were clear, though six shooters rode their hips. They seemed determined, though he was unimpressed. "Get off the road. We're running a herd of beeves to the fort and got no time for this." He started forward again, then stopped.

The smaller man, reaching down to pat his horse's withers, suddenly slid a rifle out of a scabbard and swung it in his general direction. "Maybe you didn't hear right. We're not asking you to stop. We're telling you. Some no good, cattle thieving skunks hit a herd a ways back to the east. You won't mind if we check a few brands, would you?"

A couple of Slate's gang, seeing the herd stopped and hearing the confrontation with the two armed men rode forward. See Bird continued talking. "We're giving you the chance to back down with no bloodshed. If those beeves are yours, I'll apologize and we'll all be on our way."

Blackie's eyes darted left and right. He seemed to become aware, for the first time, of his precarious position. If these men had planned an ambush, there could be no better site between here and the fort. Still, he saw no one else. They were probably bluffing. "Get outta our way," he ordered. "You touch one steer, and I'll kill you myself. I might just kill you anyhow." He turned his head to his men, who were riding up, to give an order.

"We were afraid you might not see it our way, so we brought along some support. Captain Anderson," See Bird called over his shoulder. From behind a cut bank scarcely fifty yards away wheeled, with pennants flying, a column of troopers on the walk. The stunned outlaws gaped.

Luke watched them with some amusement. Noticing one outlaw in particular, he spoke up, "Well, hello there, you yellow-bellied snake. How's your whip hand feeling these days? Beat any horses lately?"

"That's them, Blackie," the man spluttered. "They're the ones who hit us the other night." He reached across his body to cross-draw the pistol with his good hand. He never made it. Luke's .45 barked and the rider slumped in the saddle. Blackie's hand flicked to his holster. See Bird heard the lead slug from Blackie's gun thud into Luke's body, and watched as his friend slid to the ground. His Winchester responded instantly. It seemed to be the signal for all hell to break loose.

See Bird leaped from his horse and dragged Luke to one side, away from any chance of being trampled by the milling cattle, firing as he could. Bullets pinged off rocks and ripped the air. The outlaws fired a ragged volley at the advancing troopers, only to see several of their own men topple from their horses at the disciplined fire thrown back at them.

"Throw down your weapons!" Captain Anderson shouted as his men closed with the outlaws. "Do it now!"

"I'll be damned before I surrender to a bunch of nig.." Blackie aimed at the captain but never finished his statement. His body rocked from the fusillade that tore at him. The final shot seemed to throw him from the saddle.

Those bandits remaining in their saddles who could still ride, turned to flee, firing as they rode. Suddenly, from their right sprang the second platoon, guns blazing, descending a small ridge which had concealed them. Several more outlaws tumbled from their horses before the remainder, despairing of their situation, dropped their guns in the dirt and raised their hands. Quickly, Sergeant Cribbs' men rounded them up. The firing ceased as quickly as it had started.

"Lieutenant," the captain ordered, "secure the prisoners and report on casualties."

"Yes, sir!" he snapped a crisp salute.

"Luke, you just rest easy," See Bird murmured. "We're gonna get you to a doctor right soon. You'll be fine in no time." See Bird cradled his young friend's head.

"I don't know, Red. It's a powerful hurt. If I don't make it…" He wrestled with the pain a moment and then continued, "I was taking such a fancy to Mattie. You tell her I was thinking about her, will you?" When Luke tried to look up into See Bird's eyes, he shifted his weight, causing him to gasp in pain and fall back, semiconscious.

See Bird ripped open the bloodstained shirt and examined the wound. "I'm sorry, I can't do that. You'll have to do it yourself, pardner."

Captain Anderson rode up and dismounted. "How is he?" he asked.

"Hurt pretty bad, I guess. Bullet's least not hit a lung, but the wound looks dirty."

The captain nodded. "Looks like our old saw bones is going to have a busy evening. Two of our men were hit, neither serious—and Luke here. He looks the worst." He looked away a second, watching his troopers take the surviving bandits into custody. "It's a shame to waste time fixing up scum like these, only to hang them. But that's the way it is. At least we can bury seven of them here. The trap worked perfectly and I think we bagged the whole lot of 'em. It should be a bit more peaceful around here with that bunch gone. It's been a good day's work," he said with satisfaction. "Now let's get this boy to a doctor."

Old Doc Martin was the post doctor. Having seen action in Sherman's army from Shiloh to Atlanta, and then the human results of war with the plains Indians, treating six men for gunshot wounds scarcely ruffled his already crusty demeanor. He swiftly and efficiently dealt with the five lesser wounded men and then turned his attention to the man stretched out on the table before him. See Bird watched the doctor at his work, helping out as he could. The doctor's grizzled face glistened with the sweat of his labor as, hunched over the table, he cleaned, poked, and prodded around and into the ugly rip just below Luke's sternum. Finally, slowly straightening his back, he stood and wiped his gory hands on a towel. As he walked over to a basin of water to scrub his hands he said, "Mister Carpenter, I've done about all that I can for your friend here. Fortunately, the bullet didn't seem to hit any vital organ. Unfortunately, the filthy thing is still in there somewhere. It could be nearly anywhere, and I have no way of finding it. If I keep digging around in there, I'm afraid I'll kill the boy for sure."

"Will he make it?"

"Only God knows. I've seen men live long lives with more metal than that in them. But I've seen more of them die. Truth is, I just don't know." He shook his head. Luke moaned. "At least I have enough morphine to kill his pain. Look, I'm tired and need to take a break, get something to eat. You should come, too. You've been here the whole time."

See Bird's tired eyes met the doctor's. "You go on. I'll be there shortly."

Doc Martin shrugged in resignation and turned to the door. As it closed quietly behind him, See Bird approached the table. Luke moaned softly again and See Bird spoke gently. "Luke, I'm mighty sorry this thing had to happen to you. Even if you do talk more than what's good for you, you're still a man I'm proud to ride with." His black eyes grew shiny. From the nearby basin he took a damp cloth and laid it on Luke's fevered forehead. An ashen pallor covered the young man's drugged face. Blood seeping from the chest wound had already stained the gauze bandage crimson. The Indian surveyed the scene, and with a clarity of thought and certitude that brooked no doubt, he knew he was watching Luke die. And with a matching certainty, he knew he had to do something, anything to try to save him.

His eyes scanned the shadowed room, desperately searching. A roll of clean gauze lay beside the basin. He decided to replace the bandage. Carefully, he removed the bloodstained wrap. Luke's head slowly moved from side to side. How long the morphine would last was anyone's guess. Whatever See Bird was going to do, he knew it had to be soon. Blood continually trickled from the tear in Luke's chest. As See Bird reached for the clean gauze, his eyes fell on a pile of the doctor's tools. When he saw what looked like long-handled pliers, he knew exactly what he was about to attempt. Deliberately, he picked them up. He hovered for a moment over Luke's body, like a large bird seeking a place to land, becoming familiar with the feel of the tool in his hand. Then, exhaling as he would were he about to fire a rifle at a distant target, he inserted the end of the pliers in the wound.

See Bird closed his eyes and focused inwardly, on the feel of the metal as it ever so slowly nudged the disturbed and torn flesh aside, searching for what—he didn't know. He only knew that when he found the alien object he would recognize it. A groan of pain escaped Luke's lips as the pliers scraped soft tissue. Still, See Bird pressed on. In his mind's eye he saw the pliers penetrating and gently nudging its path forward. Then he paused, withdrew the pliers a fraction of an inch and moved them laterally. He felt resistance as the tip brushed something hard. It felt like a bone, but no bone should be there, closer to Luke's spine than to his chest. See Bird opened the pliers' bite and massaged the hard object, seeking for a grip.

The return journey through Luke's chest cavity seemed excruciatingly slow. Yet See Bird feared that unless he moved with what felt like agonizing slowness, he could do more damage than good. When the pliers were finally free from the young man's damaged chest, See Bird stared down at the thing in his hands, a long and bloody pair of pliers with a blunted .45 slug in its grip. Carefully he removed and examined the slug, setting down the pliers on the small table. Then he placed the slug on a small dish and flexed the cramped fingers of his left hand. He brought a basin of fresh water from the stove, and with a clean towel began swabbing the wound. It was while he was thus engaged that the door opened and Doc Martin entered.

Seeing Luke's friend cleaning the wound, he smiled and approached, only to stop short. The smile disappeared as his eyes found the small table with the bloody pliers.

The start of an angry frown was forming as he took a step and was about to speak. His frown faded and the flint in his eyes was replaced by wonder. There in a small dish by the basin lay what could only be, what must be, the nearly fatal bullet. He picked it up as if weighing it and opened his mouth but no words came. See Bird looked up and saw his confusion.

"I just couldn't sit here and watch him die, so I got it out."

"How did you? I mean how could you?" Taking a breath, he tried again. "Do you realize what you've done? Where did you learn…?" Doc Martin slumped into a chair by the table, turning the grey slug over in his hands.

See Bird stopped working on his friend. He picked up a clean towel and wiped his hands, then turned to face Doc Martin directly, speaking thoughtfully. "I never learned this. Sometimes I just know, and my hands do it. Some people say I am just lucky that way."

The old doctor watched his patient's quiet and steady breathing. "That's not luck, young man. That's a gift. My God! I can hardly believe it." He chuckled in amazement. "Mister Carpenter, I think it's time for you to go get something to eat and get some rest. I can clean up here and tend your patient 'til you return. I think he's going to be just fine now."

See Bird stepped back and dropped the cloth into the basin. His hands hung uselessly at his sides. Exhaustion swept through his body, mingled with a joy impossible to describe. He just nodded his head and turned to leave the room. As he pulled the door shut, he could hear Doc Martin whistling some nameless tune as he went about his work.

Chapter 18

See Bird spent the next two weeks handling Bar L and Double Z business while waiting for Luke to recover enough to attempt the trip home to Texas. One hundred thirty-eight of the nearly two hundred head of cattle recovered from the rustlers wore the Double Z brand. The remainder carried brands from four unfamiliar outfits, all of which must have made the trek from Texas earlier in the season. None were from the Bar L.

The telegraph from Fort Sands, Oklahoma, to Caldwell, Kansas, hummed with messages and responses to messages. Boadry was overjoyed they had recovered their cattle. When those retrieved by the Bar L were added, it turned out the Double Z was short only two head. And that was more than made up for by the selling price See Bird was able to negotiate for the cattle at Fort Sands, $10.25 a head vs. $10 per at Caldwell. It looked as though the worried trail boss was likely to keep his job after all. The remainder of the unclaimed cattle was credited to the Bar L, with See Bird and Luke receiving half the profit of their sale. When See Bird gave Luke his share, which totaled some $158, plus his wages earned for working the drive, the young man, for perhaps the first time in his life, was speechless.

Not all the news coming from "The Border Witch" was about the cattle business, however. Big Jim told of how one night the good citizens of the city stormed the jail and dragged out Buffalo Bill Brooks, a horse thief, along with two other inmates, just for good measure, and hung the lot of them. Earlier in the spring of the year, the town Marshall, along with two deputies tried to rob the bank. They, too, had been hung by a mob. As the man said, "Hell's in session" in Caldwell. The town had gone through eighteen marshals in a short period of time. So just keeping the Bar L cowhands out of trouble there seemed to be a full time job. Big Jim allowed as to how he would not miss the place and also informed the two cowhands of his decision to retire from the cattle business. He also told them that as of the day he would board the train north out of town, Slocum would be in charge. He hoped the two of them would return to Texas and continue in the employ of the Bar L. They had already become something of a legend among the men for facing down the band of rustlers and recovering the Double Z cattle. Apparently, the role the US Army played had been overlooked.

As Luke recuperated he was moved, first from a room adjoining the doctor's office to a room upstairs, and finally to the barracks, where, due to a shortage of personnel, there were many cots to choose from. The resilience of youth was never more in evidence than in his case. Day by day, color returned to his face and strength to his body. Within a week, he was up and taking short walks around the post.

See Bird tried bunking down in the barracks but gave it up after just one night and headed for the stables. After sleeping out under the stars for several months, the barracks seemed too cramped and confining. The smell of sweet hay, the peaceful sounds of horses munching oats below, the feel of the night breeze, the swing of the stars across the sky—all were music to his soul. He slept soundly.

During the day, he split his time between walking about among the settlers and the natives, listening to their stories, and sharing a bit of his when asked. He avoided the ramshackle saloons and their denizens, preferring instead the local café, 'Mom's.' The proprietor, a big-bosomed middle-aged matron, took a liking to See Bird, especially after he told her that her steak and eggs breakfast was the best he'd had since he was a child back home. After that, she made sure his plate was always full and his cup of coffee never empty. He usually spent the last of the daylight sitting in front of the barracks with Luke, whittling away with his big knife on a chunk of wood he had selected from the woodpile. Luke watched his friend slowly transform it from shapelessness into a mustachioed cavalryman straining forward, his body tense with energy, yet the reins resting comfortably in his hands.

"How long do you figure we've got to stay here, Red? I'm starting to itch for home something awful," he asked one evening.

"I guess that depends on when Doc says you can stand the ride," See Bird answered. "It looks to me that could be any day now."

"I sure hope so. You know, I've been thinking, Doc Martin told me what a close thing it was and what you done for me. And that ain't something a man can ever forget." See Bird looked at his young partner, with a twinkle in his eyes. Luke saw it and reacted. "You heard me right. And I didn't tell anyone, but I calculate while I was laying there, out to the world, I had me my sixteenth birthday. It wasn't much of a party, but at least I woke up from it. So you can call it official now. Luke Strebow is a man."

See Bird's hands didn't pause in their work. "Luke, you didn't need that birthday to become a man. The way I see it, you've been doing a man's work for a while now. But that's not all what makes a man. You found something inside yourself that tells you where you should stand, and you listen to it. Could be, it's your conscience, but I tend to believe it's something bigger. You make up your own mind after looking down the trail as far as you can, and seeing how it helps or hurts other folks as well as yourself." See Bird sighed. "I've seen many men a lot older than you who never get there, who probably will go to their graves and never spend one minute wondering how they could become the person they should be. See Bird stopped and chuckled to himself. "I apologize for running on like this, but look around you, Luke. The world is full of old boys playing at being men. The real McCoy is not so common."

The two men fell silent, sitting there on the barracks porch, letting the evening swallow them up. Aromas from the mess hall drifted on the air. Somewhere a door slammed. See Bird's knife flew like a brush in his hands as it scraped the brim of the cavalryman's hat. Luke finally broke the silence. "Red, who are you? I mean, I know you better than practically anybody, but I don't even know your real name."

"Well, that's no mystery, Luke. When I was born my mother named me after the first thing she saw. My name's

See Bird. And my twin brother's name is See Right. I don't know why she called him that."

"You've got a twin? Boy that must have been something. What's he doing now?"

The knife hesitated momentarily in See Bird's hand and then resumed its work, "I don't rightly know. A few years back we had us some hard times. My mom died, and dad sort of lost interest in things. Two hard winters, and it was only my Uncle Isaac holding things together. The place couldn't support us all, so me and See Right left. He sent a few letters from the east, and then they stopped. I headed south. That's about it. Any other questions?" he asked with a smile.

"Just one, Mr. Carpenter," Luke said playfully. "Now that I know your real name, I want to know what you would prefer. I never considered that before, and I'd like to call you as you like it best."

See Bird whittled away. "I didn't have much say in picking out my first name, and my people often change their names as they grow up. So I guess it doesn't really make much difference to me. What matters a lot more is the way a person says whichever name they choose to use. So you call me whatever you want."

"Good. Then if you don't mind, I think from now on I'm going to call you by your given name. That feels better than calling you a color." Luke laughed at his own joke and slapped his knee. See Bird chuckled as well.

A few mornings later found the two men riding their favorite mounts, leading a pair of pack horses, across a low ridge several miles to the south-east of the fort. They paused briefly to get their bearings and take a drink from their canteens. The sun was well above the horizon, and the late August day promised to be another hot one. The last of the dew had evaporated from the long grass browning as the summer waned, but the riders scarcely noticed.

"Ain't it grand, See Bird? I mean who would have ever thought that a cowhand could earn such money? I tell you the truth. Pa is going to be mighty happy to see me ride in carrying more money than he made in a year. Yes, sir. Nabbing rustlers, except for a few minor dangers, like collecting bullets, can be quite profitable."

"I suppose so. But we still have to get there, and don't forget," See Bird added, "we didn't quite get them all. Somehow, Slate wiggled away. That cat must be on his ninth life by now, and maybe someone like Taggart will do us a favor and polish him off. Somehow I doubt it though. Still, I don't expect that he'll be much of a danger now, with his gang wiped out and a price on his head." Kiamichi hopped forwards a step or two and vigorously bobbed his head up and down several times. "What's the matter, boy? Am I sitting here too long for you?" He turned to Luke and asked, "How you doing? Think you could pick up the pace a bit?"

"Hey, old timer," he laughed, "I guess I surely can. And if I die, why, you just do your magic over me again and I'll be good as new. Yes sir, I think I'll stick by you for a long time. Let's go." See Bird clicked his tongue and flicked his reins. Kiamichi broke into a fast canter. The rhythmic thudding of the horses hooves quickly faded, leaving behind only two furrows in the grass to mark their passing.

Chapter 19

Even late in the year, as low as it was, the Red River was a beautiful sight to the two weary travelers. Upstream, where they were crossing on their return trip, the river braided itself into numerous channels, all fordable, and then unwound itself again. Small scrub grew on the gravel bars, and numerous tracks of small and not so small game gave evidence to the natural life that depended on it. The two men crossed and dismounted, then unshucked their clothes. From a nearby overhanging bank they jumped into a deep pool, splashing and frolicking like the young boys they had been not so long before.

Luke showed himself to be a powerful, if somewhat inefficient, swimmer. In sprints he would surge ahead of his smaller companion, but given some distance, See Bird would consistently pull ahead of the thrashing swimmer. See Bird was pleased to see that the extra time they spent traveling slowly had paid off. Luke showed little sign of discomfort from the chest wound that had so nearly killed him.

Later, after they climbed back into their clothes, they decided this would be the perfect place to pitch camp for the night. Though it was not yet late in the evening, there was a September coolness that, coupled with their recent swimming break, made the promise of a camp fire seem especially pleasant.

"Drink up, Luke. That's the last of the coffee," See Bird said as he tossed the dregs and swished out the coffee pot. "The way the tracks run from all the outfits that crossed here earlier, I'd guess there's a road ranch nearby downstream. We'll head that way, pick up what we need, and then aim ourselves for home. I don't figure we need to head over to Fort Worth or Waco, do you?"

Luke looked thoughtful for a moment and then said, "No, I guess not. But from what the boys said on the trip north, I am a mite curious about Waco's Reservation. It'll be a shame to miss all the fun."

"Maybe. But I got a feeling when the boys leave the Reservation, they'll be a lot lighter in their wallets. I learned a long time ago that places like that tend to be rough on people like me. That, plus the fact I've never taken to alcohol much, causes me to shy away from that side of the tracks. No sir, I've got some ideas for using this money and it does not include giving it all to calico queens and card sharps."

Luke looked more closely at his companion. "I never knew you felt so strongly about it, See Bird. Those Blue Skin Presbyterians must have really got to you. We'll probably be the only drovers on the Bar L to have any money left when we get home. And you're right. Having so much money does make a man feel downright respectable, if you know what I mean. I mean if I only had my regular pay, why I might spend it all and feel mighty free and easy about it. But I got that and twice that, and you got more besides from winning in that circus. What are you planning to do with it all, anyway?"

See Bird blew a tiny chip off his carved trooper's mustache and inspected his nearly completed work. "It's not like I have real plans for it. It's more like ideas. I'm thinking it may be time for me to start figuring out how to settle down. I'd like to own a fine horse. Maybe I'd buy Kiamichi and some stock, start up a small outfit. If I work hard and play it smart, maybe I could become a cattleman, marry some nice girl and raise some kids. But I don't know. When I say it out like that, it don't sound quite so appealing as when I just dream about it. What about you?"

Luke lay back with his arms folded under his head, his friendly, open face reflecting every emotion he felt. "Now that part about marrying some nice girl, I agree with you there. And I've got just the one in mind. I never actually thought about doing anything else but settling down and running a spread. But I'll tell you one thing, my dear Mister Carpenter. You are making a big mistake."

"How so?"

Luke turned his head and looked directly at See Bird. "The way you ride, rope and shoot, you're just wasting your talent if you do as you said. I hear there's a number of Wild West Shows popping up that need hombres like you. And the money they pay is a heck of a lot better than droving. And more and more outfits are running these circuses like we put on with the Double Z, only bigger, with bigger purses. I heard about one over in Colorado and up in Montana, and another down in west Texas." He paused. "Now what do you think about that?"

See Bird looked even more pensive than usual. "I admit I've given it a thought or two. I've heard the same things. But I don't know. Seems I should be settled more. Guess

I'll think on it some more. But first, we've got to get back to the Bar L. It's gonna be different with Slocum the Big Man, but I guess he'll do," he shrugged. The conversation faded until all that could be heard was the crackling of the fire as it subsided and the gentle run of the river.

Three weeks later, the two trail-weary drovers walked their mounts up to the familiar bunkhouse and unloaded their gear. Old Les greeted them from the stoop. A general handyman, and at one time a top rider who broke both his legs in a nasty spill. One never healed right, leaving him with a perpetual limp.

"You boys look about done in. Why don't you clean up while I take care of your horses? With everybody gone, fact is there ain't much for a man to occupy his time with. You're the first ones back from the drive. I suppose you heard the news that Big Jim done sold out to Slocum and rattled off to parts unknown. Don't that just up and beat all?" Les rambled on, filling them in on all the latest news and gossip, while they politely listened and wished he would just tend the horses. At last he ran out of tidbits of news and opinions and took his leave, gathering up the reins of the horses and headed toward the corral.

Luke slapped See Bird on the back as they entered the bunkhouse. "Now that's one thing I could do without. Traveling with you I got used to a lot of quiet. I think tomorrow I'll just go a visiting the neighbors. There's a gal I would like to call on."

See Bird hesitated as if to say something, then thought better of it and said, "That sounds like a fine idea. Think I'll do some riding tomorrow, too. Something's been bothering me about the stock and I won't have a minute's rest until I check it out. Les'll just have to get by on his own for another day or two." Luke agreed with a laugh.

Chapter 20

See Bird had been riding north along the west range of the Bar L grazing range, the land that lay between it and the Double Z, looking for something but not knowing exactly what it was. It had been months since he and the young Luke Strebow had ridden the roundup. It wasn't just the temperature change from July to October that made such a difference. He had changed also. His experiences made him a warier, yet more confident man. At the same time, he was aware life was more complex and confusing than he thought previously. Try as he might to concentrate on the task at hand, Mattie O'Meara's face kept reappearing in his mind's eye—one minute smiling, open and friendly at the contest, and the next minute shocked, saddened, but still defiant, as he found her on that terrible night. She was a woman any man would be proud to have at his side, and See Bird had been thinking of calling on her himself when Luke had announced his intentions.

He had said nothing to Luke about his feelings. He was not sure why. Certainly, Mattie had never given him reason to think she was interested in him for any reason except that he could find his way around a dance floor. Still, he thought, or maybe he just imagined, there had been moments that evening when she had looked deeply into his eyes as they danced. Once, when he turned quickly from across the room, he found her hazel eyes watching him before she averted them. And was it his imagination or did she let her hand linger in his just a moment longer than was customary? What was a man supposed to think?

He shook his head as if to clear it and stared across the wide landscape as a chilly October breeze fanned his hot cheeks. The land dropped away on both sides of him as he drifted along. Certainly, any plans Slate had concocted had come crashing down about his head. With his gang destroyed and him on the run, perhaps See Bird was worried about nothing. But three things kept his eyes roving the landscape: First, Slate had dropped off the map. No one knew where he was. And no one knew how deeply he had woven his web, or if other men were following his orders. Secondly, See Bird never understood why Slate set up shop down here in the first place. If he wanted to rustle the herd on the long drive, he could have waited in Oklahoma for it to come to him. And thirdly, he had found out, by asking around, that no Bar L drovers had been up to the northwest corner of the range to drive out any cattle, and that drovers from the Double Z told him that to the best of their recollection, Morgan, Buck, and Turpin had worked that area. It was not a smoking gun but it all made him mighty uneasy.

He rode on, seeing nothing out of the ordinary. That night found him at the north end of the range, making camp where he and Luke had done so months before, by the small stream in the cottonwoods. Even though he brought coffee and the night wind was chilly, he chose to make no fire, but sat huddled with his back to a rock, a saddle blanket over his shoulders, eating some biscuits and cold meats that Juanna carefully packed for him. As he washed his makeshift supper down with fresh stream water, he wondered to himself why he was being so secretive. He had examined the area carefully. Clearly, there was no one within miles, and yet he could not shake the sensation of being watched. As he drifted off to sleep he wondered if perhaps his anxiety over Mattie was not affecting his judgment on other things. Some coffee would have tasted mighty good, and a fire is a comforting thing somehow. He dozed and drifted in and out of sleep. Yes, a fire sure would have felt good. Suddenly, he sat bolt upright. He smelled smoke.

To be honest it was only the faintest whiff of smoke. And See Bird knew that out here, depending on the vagaries of the wind currents, the odor of burning wood could carry for miles. Perhaps it was only some lonesome, wandering cowboy like himself, returning from some distant errand. Perhaps, but See Bird didn't believe it for a minute. This place was too far off the beaten path. To the north lay a stretch of land that was inhospitable to travelers for tens of miles and increasingly unsuitable for grazing cattle. It was a country, crisscrossed by eroded land, dry gulches, arroyos, and little game. The general boundary of the Bar L spread lay here for just that very reason. To the west the land claimed by the Double Z ended as well, though from its northern boundary the land was more open. That was why the long drive had run west before it turned north.

See Bird had thoroughly scouted out the land to the east when he and Luke had been drifting the stock down for the roundup. If someone had made a camp to his north, it was because he did not want company. Perhaps there was a good reason. In the dark, See Bird carefully dug his moccasins from his saddlebags and tucked his riding boots away. After sliding his knife behind his left hip, he strapped on the right-handed holster for the Colt .45 and removed the rifle scabbard containing the Winchester from his saddle. Lest the metal barrel scrape or knock against some rock, he decided to leave it in its sheath. Thus armed, he considered his best course of action.

Fortunately, See Bird had been blessed with keen night vision. That, along with the light cast by a nearly three-quarter full moon, insured that he could move stealthily and surely. While he could have waited until morning light, he was afraid by then the fire would be out and whoever made it would be long gone. Besides that, with all his nerves keyed up the way they were, rolling over and going back to sleep just was not an option.

The small gravelly stream flowed west to east and several miles away joined its waters to a larger stream that flowed generally south. The steep wooded ridge that ran along its north bank provided an effective barrier to cold northern winds and to any wandering stock as well. See Bird worked his way slowly down the stream, using his eyes, ears, and nose to detect anything out of the ordinary. But beyond the murmuring of the stream and the not too distant yip of a coyote there was nothing to be heard. The brief aroma of wood smoke that had so startled him never repeated itself. Yet he never once questioned its reality.

Having worked his way as far down stream as he thought possible for smoke to carry and having seen, heard, and smelled nothing, he started to work back up on the other side. Occasional outcroppings of rocks and detritus of old landslides, mingled with rough brush made this a tiring exercise, and just as fruitless. He returned to within several hundred yards of where he had begun, and the excitement he first felt had disappeared. His long day's ride and interrupted sleep, coupled with this midnight hike, had taken its toll on his energy. With a sigh of resignation he stepped back into some low vegetation which offered the promise of at least a little shelter from the chilly wind before he would continue on to his camp site. Morning would come soon enough. He decided he would have to continue the search then.

He nearly lost his balance as the small tree he leaned against for support collapsed into a narrow corridor between two low walls of rock. The gap was artfully concealed and scarcely wide enough to allow for a set of long horns to pass between. A small dry wash which most likely had carried water in the spring spilled to the stream along which See Bird had been prowling.

The narrow black corridor held no appeal for him. It would undoubtedly be blocked at the other end and watched as the most likely entrance for unwelcome visitors. Also, the loose rock that had washed or tumbled down, nearly closing the gap, looked treacherous to negotiate silently, especially at night. Carefully, he replaced the tree and the disturbed underbrush, and more silently than before, sidled to his left, his eyes searching for another route in, for he knew that a man as wary as Slate would always plan an escape route.

Dawn found See Bird huddled behind a large boulder overlooking the northwest rim of the box canyon. From his vantage point, he could understand now why Slate had chosen the Double Z and Bar L to rustle. Situated at the northernmost end of both ranches, and bordering on its north miles of trackless wasteland, it was ideally situated for his illicit purposes. See Bird wondered how long it took Slate to put all the pieces in place before he made his move. Such an enterprise could not have been done in a single season. Built into the east wall of the canyon were a small lean-to cabin and a corral with sheds. From almost anywhere else along the rim they would have been invisible. Between the cabin and the sheds was a small pool near the base of the wall. Clearly, the canyon was spring fed with no outlet visible save the camouflaged one See Bird had stumbled upon. And that freshet probably carried only the spring melt and occasional summer downpour. Sparse cattle grazed lazily. Just as clearly, this was not a place large enough for rustled stock to be kept for much longer than it took to collect, rebrand, and move them on to market. Once See Bird had settled in, he studied every inch of the canyon walls, searching for a rear exit. It had to be steep enough to deter unwatched cattle from escaping, yet safe enough for them to be driven out. For while the narrow entrance See Bird stumbled into might be useful for bringing in a few head at a time, any attempt to move a large number out of the canyon in that direction would have left tracks no one could have missed, even in the dark.

Finally, he found it. On the north east wall, what looked like a scar, turned out, on closer study to be a well-used gully that angled from the rim to a clump of trees just north of the sheds. Now that he understood the layout of the hideaway, See Bird made himself as comfortable as possible. The only thing left was for him to locate and count the outlaws.

The October sun climbed slowly above the rim, and See Bird had to fight drowsiness as best he could. Finally, the cabin door opened and a balding man in his woolens stepped out and tossed a basin of water over the railing. Not a wisp of smoke curled out of the chimney. They must have killed the fire last night. That was probably when he caught wind of it. Slate was being very cautious, if he was even there. See Bird thought he detected movement at the cabin's lone window. Clearly, someone else was stirring around. A few minutes later, the cabin door swung open and another man fully dressed this time emerged, stretched, and turned toward the corral. Shortly after that he returned with two saddled horses, tied them at the rail, and reentered the cabin. See Bird now had to make another decision. It appeared the two rustlers were the only residents and they would not be there much longer. He could go back and report to the authorities what he had found. He was disappointed the ringleader of the gang did not seem to be present. But, See Bird considered, the man still might be nearby. If so, then these two men might very well know his whereabouts. If See Bird could get them to talk, the outlaw chief may yet be captured. After all the pain the man had caused, the young drover decided he could not let these two go and risk the escape once more of their leader.

His decision thus made, See Bird began the arduous task of working his way down the slope and onto the canyon floor. It seemed to take forever to negotiate the broken terrain. Once, rushing from one boulder to another, a foot slipped and his rifle rapped against the rock. He was grateful for the leather scabbard, which muffled the sound.

At last, he found himself only slightly above the canyon floor and to the north of the cabin. He could scarcely approach across the open canyon, and this way afforded the most protection on his approach. Also, if the riders did try to leave, this northern approach would give him the best chance to intercept them.

Though it was October and he was without a coat, See Bird felt the sweat of nervous exertion on his neck. He paused to catch his breath and wipe his face with the back of his hand. He found he had been holding his breath and forced himself to inhale deeply several times. He estimated the cabin was now just several hundred yards away. And, except for the final stretch, there appeared to be good cover all the way. Nevertheless, he knew it was vital for his safety that he use all the skill he possessed to remain undetected. Having rested for a minute, he once again disappeared back into the landscape.

After what seemed an eternity, See Bird found himself peering across the open space that lay between him and the cabin, a distance of no more than thirty feet. There was still no sign of Slate. Where was the man? As he was wondering, the cabin door opened and the two men he had seen earlier, both now fully dressed and armed, stepped down to the rail where their two mounts stood. One patted his pockets as if looking for the makings of a smoke.

See Bird was disappointed. Clearly, the two were merely hangers-on. Slate's toughest men had ridden with the gang broken up by the cavalry. Most likely, these two had been left behind to keep an eye on things until Slate's return, an event that now seemed unlikely. He considered again letting them ride away. Most likely they knew nothing, but then he decided to stick with his plan. They were cattle rustlers and should pay for their crimes. In any case the cattle in the canyon had to be reclaimed. He unsheathed the rifle, dropped its scabbard, and stepped out from the trees.

He had not taken three steps before a voice to his immediate left barked, "Hold it right there, redskin. I've been waiting for you." Slate chuckled to himself and cocked his revolver. "You two saddle tramps get yourselves over here and see how a mousetrap works." The speaker stepped from behind a low rock wall, nonchalantly waving his pistol. He walked up until he was only about ten feet distant then stopped and leveled the revolver at See Bird's face while, at the same time, leaning against a tree. He was the very picture of arrogance. And ruefully, See Bird acknowledged to himself that he had every right to be confident. "Now I'd be very much obliged if you toss that rifle to the side and drop your gun belt." See Bird obeyed. "That's a real good boy. Now kick it off to the side." See Bird did as he was ordered. He knew that whether or not he survived the next thirty seconds was completely out of his hands.

"Seth, Jud, take a good long last look at a real pain in the neck. This red nigger has ruined plans I worked on for months. I promise he'll die real slow, Injun style." Both men looked uncomfortable to See Bird. They had hired on for easy money, picking off some cattle here and there. It wasn't that they had moral qualms about killing a man. Jud had a reputation as a bushwhacker, not entirely deserved. He had killed one man in an ambush, but he had never been charged. Seth had not even accomplished that much. They were two-bit players in the scheme of things and they knew it.

See Bird knew he had to stall, to play for time. "Slate, it's all over. Your gang is dead or busted up. These two drifters are all you've got left, and from the looks of things, they'd like to be just about anywhere but here. Back at the ranch they know where I've gone, and if I'm not back tomorrow, they'll come looking." He put his hands on his hips, assuming as relaxed an air as he could. His index finger brushed the hilt of his knife. "Whether you kill me or not, the result will be the same, except for one thing. Now they'll want you and these two boys for murder. And the law won't quit until you and they hang." See Bird turned his head slightly to better face the two would-be bad men. "Odds are good there're no posters out for you two, yet. But you ride the owl-hoot trail with this man, and I promise it'll be a short one, and its end won't be pretty."

Seth licked his lips nervously and spoke, "What he says makes sense, boss. Let's just tie him up and ride out of here." Jud nodded his agreement and shifted from foot to foot with anxiety.

"Don't either of you two move a muscle until I say so," Slate responded angrily. "I've just let this fool talk so I can show him what a fool he is before he dies." He turned his attention back to his prisoner. "You see, Injun boy, I knew you and that wet nosed pup that rides with you got back to the ranch. I got me a friend at the telegraph office in Mingo that let's me know of people's comings and goings around here. And I don't hear me no puppy yapping, now do you boys?" Slate laughed at his own hilarity. "If he'd a'knowed where you was going he'd damn sure fasten his neck to your chain. No, he's probably off sparkin' that little Irish whore. He ain't thinking about you, and there ain't nobody else down at the ranch except an old Mexican cook and a cripple. I just don't see how either of them will come a riding to your rescue. Do you, boys? No, indeed. Yesterday I seen you riding in from up on the rim and when I figured you were too dumb to find this place, I even lit a little fire for you. Now wasn't that smart?"

He glanced at Seth and Jud for just a moment, dragging his pistol's aim from See Bird's face. Moving instantly, See Bird's left hand dug his big knife from the sheath behind his hip and launched it with a powerful underhand throw. In almost the same motion he dove to his right, rolling on the ground, grasping for his Colt. A bullet ripped the air near his head as he heard the knife thud into the tree behind Slate. Afraid he had missed the mark, he frantically yanked the gun from its holster, expecting at any second to feel an angry bullet crash into his body. It never arrived. Instead, when he raised his eyes above his pistol, he saw the two drifters frozen as if paralyzed, staring at their leader.

Slate was still leaning against the tree. See Bird's knife had deeply embedded itself in the trunk But it had not missed its mark. Passing cleanly through the man's neck, it had impaled him there. The revolver still hung in his clenched hand. His pale-faced head was cocked slightly off to one side, his horrified eyes frozen open in death's stare, his mouth hung open in a silent scream. His front was bathed in red, and a small stream of his life blood still flowed and pooled at his feet.

"Don't shoot, Mister! For God's sake, don't shoot!" Seth begged. The terrified men couldn't take their eyes from the grotesque scene that presented itself. "All we done was mind the place and care for the stock. Please take them all," he whimpered. "Just let us go."

"Your guns!" See Bird waved the Colt and stood. As quickly as they could, the two men unbuckled their belts and dropped them in the dirt. "I oughta turn you in. But I'm gonna give you twenty-four hours first. Now mount up and get out of here. If I so much as see you flinch, I'll kill you," he threatened. See Bird stooped and retrieved his Winchester, levering a round into the chamber. He tucked the Colt into his belt and said to the hesitant rustlers, "Don't test me. I know the business end of a rifle. Move!" The drifters took him at his word and scurried to their horses.

Throwing one last look at Slate's impaled corpse and the Indian pointing a rifle in their direction, Seth and Jud dug in their spurs and drove their horses up the gully and out of the canyon. See Bird had a feeling they would not stop until they were as far away from here as possible.

Slowly, he turned, picked up the rifle scabbard and slipped the Winchester back in. Then he stepped over to the tree and worked his knife out of the trunk and from Slate's neck. As the body slumped to the ground, See Bird suddenly felt dizzy. A wave of nausea threatened momentarily to engulf him. He steadied himself and said, "Well, Slate, I finally saw you hung, but I didn't expect it to be on the business end of a knife. I should let you rot, but that wouldn't be the Christian thing to do, now would it?" He dragged the body over to the gully and leaned as hard as he could against the rock wall Slate had surprised him from. It stood for a moment and then slowly gave way, tumbling over and covering the body.

He shuffled past the cabin and down to the narrow canyon entrance he discovered just the night before. *Had it only been last night?* he wondered. It felt like weeks. He knew he was suffering from lack of sleep, lack of food, and far too much activity. His body's needs were demanding attention. He quickly cleared the brush away from the entrance and whistled. He was answered by a whinny. As Kiamichi nickered, See Bird wound a hand in his mane and slipped a leg over his back. He patted the stout-hearted pony's shoulder. "Let's pick up our gear and go home, boy," he said.

Chapter 21

It was a couple weeks later and mid-October when the chuck wagon, preceded by Slocum and most of the boys, rattled up to the ranch. Luke and See Bird were almost used to having the bunk house to themselves. But now, even with the return of the Bar L crew, there were empty cots. Some men had taken their pay and moved on. Others had gone to their homes until next spring's roundup would come calling again. It became Luke's responsibility to tell See Bird's story, for when the Choctaw drover was asked about it, he would be more likely to shrug and continue whittling on another yet formless chunk of wood than answer.

To tell the truth, See Bird was much more concerned about the future than he was the past. As the days shortened and cooled, once the ranch chores were done, activities tended to move indoors. Poker became the usual way to pass an evening. After partying in Caldwell and Waco, many of the cowhands didn't have a tail feather left and those who still had money were free with their wagers. Tempers could flare, but calmer heads always prevailed. See Bird didn't bet. As he explained to Luke one evening, after the young man had lost some money on a 'sure bet,' "The surest way to double your money is to fold it over." Evenings would more likely find him sitting on his cot in his stocking feet, working that blade on wood. Luke began to spend more of his time on the road. One evening he returned, as usual, but it was clear from his sour mood that he was not happy. He pulled up a stool by See Bird's cot and sat.

"I tell you, pardner, I just don't understand women. Maybe I never will," he said in frustration.

See Bird stopped his carving. "Now what's brought this on? I see you ride out of here all smiles, and come back looking like you wrestled with a grizzly—and lost."

"Oh, See Bird," he sighed. "It's that Mattie O'Meara. You know I've been courting her. And she's friendly as all get out, but every time I work up the nerve to ask her if she'll be my girl, she changes the subject or finds something else she's got to do. I feel like giving up after a while. So I get back on my horse to leave, and suddenly she's leaning on my leg and begging me to drop by again. I feel so whipsawed I don't know which way to turn." See Bird laughed sympathetically. Luke continued, "She's always welcoming to me, invited me to supper even. But heck, she's that same way with most everybody."

See Bird planted his feet on the floor and said with a smile, "Well, maybe I should drop in on her and have a chat."

"That's a great idea, See Bird. She asks about you every time I go down there, what you're up to and all. Maybe you could find out what she's thinking and help me out."

"Luke," his friend replied, "I don't believe there is a man alive who can find out what a woman is thinking if she don't want him to. But I would be happy to pay Mattie a visit. I just haven't wanted to step on your toes."

Sunday morning found See Bird up early, scrubbing the caked mud off his boots and donning his clean best shirt and woolen vest. He tied a red bandana around his neck, stuck a colorful turkey feather in the brim of his tall black hat, and with a jaunty air, swung onto Kiamichi's back and headed down the road toward Rimes.

Buckboards were still pulling up to the little white Methodist church when he rode in. Sunday morning church-going was more than a bunch of silent folks listening to a dry sermon delivered by a long faced preacher. It was a time for families who lived miles distant from one another to rekindle relationships and share gossip. See Bird took a seat in a rear pew, hoping to catch a glimpse of Mattie. She told him her family were Catholic, but since the nearest Catholic Church was a little Mexican chapel twice as far away, her parents said as to how they believed the Good Lord probably wouldn't mind so much if they worshipped with neighbors, at least occasionally. And there she was four pews ahead on the other side of the aisle. *There is no way a person could miss her*, he thought to himself, *even in a crowd*. See Bird was surprised that he actually found himself paying attention to the sermon. The pastor was a curly haired middle aged man who spoke with considerable conviction and enthusiasm about reaping what you sow. Now that was something See Bird concurred with wholeheartedly.

Following the closing hymn, See Bird edged toward the door and greeted Mattie and her family as they passed. Mattie's father spoke first. "Good morning, Mister

Carpenter. It's good to see you here. I didn't know you were a Methodist."

"Actually, sir, I was raised in the Presbyterian Church. I wasn't even aware of all these pieces to Christianity 'til I left home."

"Yes, well we're not Methodists either," he admitted. "But if the church is teaching from the Good Book, that's good enough for me. But I don't expect you rode all this way just to talk religion with me. Am I right?"

See Bird chuckled nervously and twisted the brim of the hat in his hands. "No sir, I didn't, and yes, sir, you are. I was wondering if I might have a minute of Mattie's time."

"Of course. Mother, you come with me and the boys to get the buckboard. We'll give you two a few minutes. Come along, boys," he said and led his family away. But now that he had Mattie to himself, See Bird suddenly felt at a loss for words.

They walked a few awkward steps together. Mattie broke the ice. "I'm mighty glad you came here today, Red. I've been wondering about you for ages. Luke's told me what you've been up to, and I just don't know what to think. How are you?"

"Oh, I'm fine, Mattie. I was talking with Luke last night, and he mentioned you." See Bird stopped short and stepped off the path. "Mattie, I need to talk with you about something serious. Will you hear me out?"

The young woman looked into his eyes and the smile disappeared from her lips, which she now firmly set in an earnest, if no less appealing look. "Of course, Red. I'll listen." She took both his hands in hers.

Her reaction gave him heart and he plunged ahead. "Mattie, I've never met any woman who rides my dreams the way you do." He almost panicked when he saw her eyes grow even bigger, but he continued. "Please hear me out all the way. I've got a little stake saved up, enough to make a start. I'd be a good man to you and never do wrong by you. I'm not proposing right now, I don't think. Maybe I am. Heck, I don't even have a ring. But don't you think I could at least come a courting so's you and I can get to know each other better? And then you could decide."

Mattie shook her head at this rambling explosion of words. He was afraid she would laugh at his clumsiness. Instead, when she looked up at him her eyes were moist. The chilly wind blew a vagrant red lock across her forehead. Absently, See Bird gently stroked it aside. His fingers lingered, and then his palm caressed her cheek before he reluctantly withdrew his hand. "Oh, mister, I love it when you touch me. It's like a burning ember on my skin. No man ever did that to me before. It makes me feel all right and peaceful somehow." Mattie took a deep breath and braced herself for what she had to say next. "But Red, look at you."

See Bird was stunned. "Mattie, if this is about me being an Indian…"

"Oh, for heaven's sake, Red," she interrupted. "That's not it at all." Her tone became gentler. "I mean, look at you—inside—where you got all your wants and dreams. You say I'm part of that now, but what about next spring? Red, I need a man who'll always be here, a steady man to take my side and be a father for my kids, a man who'll always be riding in the buggy with me." She shivered involuntarily. A specter seemed to cloud her eyes for a moment. Then she continued. "You just spent months riding about the country, shooting people and getting shot at. And you love it. It shows. To be who God made you to be, you've got to be able to follow that wanderlust. But I couldn't stand that kind of life, always watching you ride off, not knowing when or if you'll return. It'd kill me."

Her words cut like a knife. See Bird could not meet her eyes. "Red, I want you more than I've ever wanted any man in my life. But, can't you see, that's not enough." Tears were starting to roll down her cheeks. "Look inside, Red. Look deep. You're an honest man, the best I've ever known. Don't lie to yourself. Maybe you could give it all up for one or two years. Maybe you could give it up forever. But as the years pass, you'd become bitter and resentful at losing your dreams because of me. And I'd become nasty and guilty for making you give them up. And one day you'd curse me for what I did and yourself for what you'd become." She stopped, on the verge of sobbing. "Tell me I'm wrong. Tell me what I said is wrong, Red and I'll take it all back."

See Bird had never felt more miserable in his life. What had he been thinking to force himself on this woman? Her words struck hard, like body blows. But they rang true. The life he had to lead was not the life for her. And the life she had to lead was drawing steadily away from him. He knew this, and the pain it caused cut to his marrow. "Mattie, I'm so sorry," was all he could say as he took her in his arms, cupping and stroking the back of her head, winding his fingers in her curls, memorizing them forever. He held her as he had dreamed of holding her, and he knew that from today on, he would only hold her in his dreams.

She moaned as she leaned against his chest and wrapped her arms about his narrow waist. "I knew it from the start, from that day you gave me the little horse. I knew it then." She paused, "But at least I got this much of you forever. Now Red," she braced herself and pushed herself away with effort, "I think it's time for you to leave. I've got to help Ma prepare Sunday dinner." She stood on tiptoe and brushed his lips with hers. He inhaled her scent. Then she pivoted and strode purposefully to the buckboard drawn up outside the picket fence. See Bird nearly called after her, but instead watched mutely as she climbed into the buggy. He returned her farewell wave and watched until the buggy turned a corner and disappeared. A sad smile creased the corners of his mouth as he walked toward Kiamichi. Oh, that Texas could make such a woman.

Epilogue

See Bird walked down the riverboat ramp, toting his saddle and war bag. His hard body ached from years of rodeoing and riding the wide country. He had come east with the vague notion of finding his brother. At least that's what he told himself. A deeper part of himself was drawn to this land of forests and rivers east of the mighty Mississippi, a land that his people seldom spoke of but with longing, another land he had never seen.

Striding with that distinctive cowboy gait down the ramp, his saddle thrown over one shoulder, See Bird surveyed the country before him. The green mountains reared muscular backs up into an azure sky dotted with cotton-ball clouds. Dark shadows in the mountains hinted of vales and brooks that could delight and refresh the spirit. He could feel the crowfeet at the corners of his eyes relaxing as he took in the richness of the landscape. It was a beautiful land. At his feet the muddy Ohio, paying no heed, continued its eternal journey west.

He had debarked at Huntington because it was about as far east as he was prepared to go. A bustling city named by an egotistical railroad tycoon of the same name, it boasted a railroad line that could make connections to practically anywhere, and that, he thought wryly, may be just what he would do. Though years had passed, he had never erased the image of a girl far away, a girl who by now was undoubtedly a wife and mother. He could imagine Mattie standing at a ranch house door brushing one of her wayward curls out of her eyes, looking west. He sighed. It was funny though, he thought, how time had turned a painful memory into such a sweet treasure.

People hurried by him on unknown errands. Only once or twice did the appearance of this out of place cowboy elicit a furtive glance. Mostly he was just ignored. "Excuse me, miss," he spoke to a young woman as she approached. "Could you direct me to the train depot? I'm new to these parts." 'Miss,' he observed, may have been the wrong thing to say. A small girl, probably no more than two years old, clung to her long skirts.

"The depot," she said as if it were a novel thought. "I surely can tell you how to get there, but I can also tell that you've been traipsing about for a long time now." Her hazel eyes sparked with a lively sense of humor. He also thought he detected some hurt behind them. "I'll tell you what. I'll do better than that. I'm headed that way, and I'll take you there if you buy me a cup of coffee." She stood with her feet apart and hands on her hips. Strands of hair the color of flax hung from her flowered bonnet. The little girl peeked out from behind her skirts.

See Bird smiled. "That's a right nice invitation. I could use a cup of Arbuckle's myself." He was fascinated by her. Never had he met such a contradictory person. She couldn't have stood more than an inch above five feet and looked frail as a reed. Yet everything about her spoke of strength, directness, and depth of spirit.

She turned and started to walk away, with the child skipping at her side, and then stopped so suddenly he nearly collided with her. She seemed to take no notice. "I guess, as long as we're going to share each other's company for a bit, we should exchange names. "I'm Sally. This is Gertrude."

See Bird considered his response for a split second. 'Red' was how everybody seemed to know him. "See Bird," he said. "My name's See Bird Carpenter. It's a pleasure to meet you, Sally." He set down his saddle and extended his hand.

She smiled a smile that shined into dark places he didn't think would ever see the sun again and shook it. Her hand was small in his, but her grip was firm. Their eyes met and she found she was holding her breath. Then she released his hand and turned. Sally spoke over her shoulder as she set off. "You'll have to walk fast to keep up with me, Bird."

"Bird," Gertrude laughed. "That's funny."

See Bird strode along smiling to himself. Yeah, he thought, life sure is funny.

-The End-

Afterword

See Bird Carpenter was a real person. A Choctaw Indian from the 'Nations,' he drifted to West Virginia around the turn of the twentieth century, and married Sally Ethel Lambert, a young widow with a small daughter. With their combined money, they bought a 'farm' nearby, and there they lived until the 1950s, shortly before See Bird passed away. The bird-hunting incident that opens the novel, where See Bird shoots a pheasant with his index finger, is sworn to by my father. He was there.

There was nothing a person could make with his hands that See Bird could not make. At a time when almost all rural folks had outhouses, he constructed and installed indoor plumbing on their 'farm,' which was a place for raising animals, but few if any crops. He played the harmonica and could clog up a storm dancing. Every year at the county fair he would dress up in full western regalia, chaps and the black slouch hat, and bust broncs. The show never really got started until See Bird made his entrance. Sally could never stand to watch him ride but would avert her eyes until he was done. Also at the fair he would sell, for $5 each, small western carvings he made by hand.

To say they lived on the 'farm' would be the truth and yet less than the truth. Every year, when spring time arrived, See Bird would pack his "war bag" and disappear, to go rodeoing for a while. Sally never knew when he would return, though they would spend many an hour afterwards talking of his experiences. He worked the rodeo circuit for years, out to Colorado for "Cowboy Christmas," up to

Montana, and back through the Dakotas. But he never went back to Texas. He never spoke of why that was, just that it was.

In all respects Sally was a remarkable woman. A daughter of the mountains, she was the niece of Devil Anse (Anderson) Hatfield, of the famous Hatfield-McCoy feud. Devil Anse taught her to ride and shoot when she could barely sit a horse, and when the rifle kick would knock her over. But that is another story. (**Hills Aflame**, forthcoming book.) Perhaps the most remarkable thing about their love story is that she never clung to See Bird. She never tried to keep him from disappearing year after year, though as she said, she "loved to see that man come walking up the lane." She "missed him too much to tell," and besides, when he returned at the end of the summer he "always had a big wad of money he won rodeoing." There were rumors that See Bird had another love out west, perhaps even another wife. But if Sally knew, she never shared. Watch for these adventures in the upcoming title, **Up Harvey's Creek**.

When they finally sold the farm and moved into Huntington, See Bird set up a blacksmith shop behind the house where he would putter for hours, repairing and making everything from small furniture to gorgeous hand-tooled chaps, "bat wings," he called them. A small boy would stand silently, in awe, watching his magic hands work for as long as the old man would allow, perhaps handing to See Bird a small tool, or just watching the sparks fly from the whetstone wheel.